D0336733

PRAISE FOR *MY FRENCH WHORE: A LOVE STORY*

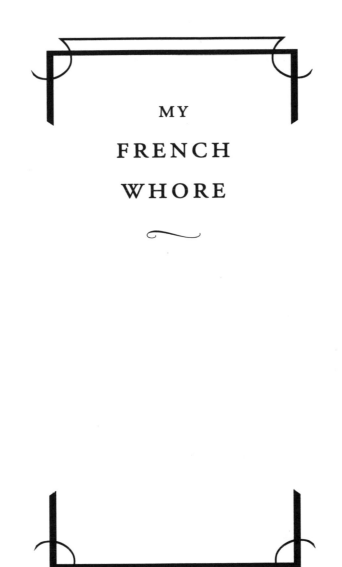

MY
FRENCH
WHORE

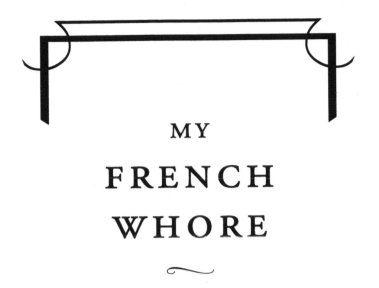

MY
FRENCH
WHORE

Gene Wilder

OLD STREET PUBLISHING
London

First published in the United Kingdom in 2007 by
Old Street Publishing Ltd, 14 Bowling Green Lane,
London EC1R 0BD, UK
www.oldstreetpublishing.co.uk

First published in the United States in 2007 by
St Martin's Press,

ISBN13: 978 1 905847 08 2
10 9 8 7 6 5 4 3 2 1

Printed by Creative Print and Design, Wales

To Karen Wilder, the heart and part of the personality
of any love story I write
&
To Elizabeth Beier, my editor, who always seems to know
when and how and what to say

Dear Captain Harrington,

I was going to burn all of this—I thought I was writing it just to help me stay sane, but then I realised the real reason was because I wanted you to understand why I did so many strange things. I hope this notebook reaches you one day, after the war. I hope you'll remember me kindly.

With great respect,
Private Peachy

MY
NOTEBOOK

ONE

⌒

MARCH, 1918

I USED TO BE A CONDUCTOR ON THE TRAIN THAT RAN back and forth from Milwaukee to Chicago. Two or three times a year I acted in our local community theatre, playing small roles mostly, but occasionally I was given a featured role. When the Milwaukee Players were putting on a play called *A Brave Coward,* by Winslow Clarke, I was given the part of a cowardly soldier during the Civil War who chooses, for the first time, to do something heroic. This was the biggest role our director had ever given me.

Our community theatre gave only three performances

for each of our plays, and on the last night of *A Brave Coward* I was in the men's dressing room applying some Skolgie's theatrical glue onto a moustache I'd made out of crepe hair, pressing it hard above my upper lip, when our director walked in. His name was John Freidel, but all the actors called him "sir" because we were a little afraid of him.

He walked past the other men, who were getting into costumes and going over their lines, and came up to my chair. "You're late, Peachy," he said.

"Sorry, sir, I came right from work. The train was late."

"Sir" could be very sarcastic when he was giving notes, but I hadn't heard him yell at anyone yet. He was a tall man and I thought his knee would hurt when he kneeled down next to me on the hard wooden floor, but I certainly wasn't going to interrupt him. He spoke confidentially, but he was very intense.

"You've been way too soft these last few nights, Paul. Terribly gentle and polite. A coward isn't a coward all the goddamn time, you know? You're starting to act like you're scared to death. Will you loosen up for me tonight?"

"I'll try, sir," I said.

"When the curtain goes up, forget the goddamn audience! Pretend it's just a rehearsal. Will you do that for me,

Paul?"

"I'll try."

Twenty minutes later my heart was in my throat. I heard the stage manager whisper "Go!" and the curtain went up. There was silence for a moment as the audience waited, and then the first line was spoken.

Thank goodness the play went well, and I know the audience liked me because they clapped especially loud when I took my bow during the curtain calls. I looked out into the audience while I was bowing and saw our director sitting in the front row. He gave me a smile and a little nod of approval.

When the play was over I kept my moustache on, which I had purposely made the colour of my wife's auburn hair. I kept trying to picture Elsie when she saw it. Elsie and I had only been married for four and a half years, but the romantic part of our relationship seemed to have faded away, like the yellow roses in our backyard at the end of summer. I lived with Elsie and her mother in three rooms on the second floor of a small but clean house in the German-Polish section of Milwaukee.

On the bus ride home a pretty girl and a soldier were sitting across the aisle from me, holding hands. The girl smiled at me. Without thinking, I touched my moustache and smiled back at her. Her boyfriend turned and gave me a hard stare. I dropped my head, pretending to be reading my theatre program.

When I got home I raced up the stairs and unlocked the kitchen door. There was a soft light coming from the half-open door of our bedroom. I stuck my head into the doorway.

"Look who's here!" I said, as rakishly as I could. Elsie was asleep, propped up against two big pillows, her long auburn hair spread out around her. A gas lamp was burning on the nightstand. The sound of my voice woke her.

"Oh, Paul," she said, still half asleep.

"I'm sorry, honey—I didn't know you were sleeping. How do you feel?"

"I was waiting up, and then I just dozed off," she said.

I made a tiny leap, trying to feature my moustache. "Look who's here!" I said.

"What time is it?" Elsie asked, trying to see the little table clock on my side of the bed.

"It must be a little past ten," I said. "How do you feel, Elsie?"

"Is my mother's light out?" she asked.

There wasn't any light coming from the adjoining bedroom.

"Yes, it's out," I said.

Still trying to get Elsie to notice my moustache, I made

another little John Barrymore leap in the air and said,

"Look who's here, Elsie."

"Paul, if you're going to eat something, please hurry."

"I'm not hungry, Elsie."

"You must be starving," she said.

"No, I had something on the train. Honestly, I'm not hungry. How do you feel?"

"If you cared how I felt, would you have left me tonight?"

"Well . . . I did care, even though I left, so the answer must be 'Yes.' You look so pretty with your hair that way."

"I don't feel pretty."

"Isn't life funny, because you do look so pretty?"

"Thank you."

I walked up and sat beside her on the bed. "I brought you something, sweetheart."

"You didn't bring me another pastry?" she asked. "Oh, Paul, why do you do that?"

"It must be love," I said, taking her hand.

"You've still got make-up all over your face. Did you know that?"

"I must have forgotten—I was so excited after the play, and I wanted to get home before you went to sleep."

I leaned down and kissed her, then took off my trousers

and underwear and socks, leaving on my shirt. I turned down the lamp and got into bed.

"Don't touch me like that, Paul."

"Why?"

"I don't feel like it," she said.

"Why?"

Elsie turned away. I lay next to her for a while, until I finally fell asleep.

The next morning I was punching tickets on the ride back to Milwaukee. The car was stuffed with soldiers and their girlfriends or wives. Mostly girlfriends, I think. Standing or seated, all the couples seemed to be kissing. A few of the older men and women were trying not to look. As I walked down the aisle my attention was caught by a passenger's newspaper.

SIX THOUSAND GERMAN GUNS OPEN FIRE AT 4:50
A.M.
2,500 BRITISH GUNS REPLY.

FRANCE WAITS FOR YANKS

After repeating "Tickets please" three times to one passionately kissing couple, I lost heart for punching tickets. When we reached the Third Street station in Milwaukee, I hopped off the passenger steps onto the station platform and helped some of the older people get off the train. Then I made my way through the crowd. Most everyone was hugging and kissing their loved ones goodbye. A little girl was clutching her mother's leg while the mother was squeezing her husband's waist as she kissed him. I stood and watched the three of them for a moment. That afternoon I wrote a letter to my wife.

> *Dear Elsie:*
> *I've joined the army. I don't think*
> *you'll ever be happy with me, and I know that*
> *I'm terribly unhappy. I've left you all of the*
> *money we have in our savings account, and I've*
> *paid the next three months of rent.*
> *Mr. Kazinsky says that you and your mother*
> *can have your old jobs back at the bakery, if you*
> *wish.*
>
> > *Good-bye,*
> > *Paul*

TWO

⌒

I WAS SENT TO CAMP PIKE, NEAR LITTLE ROCK, ARKANSAS.
On our third day of basic training, I was assigned to
Company B. I can't say that I loved basic training, but I
did find two good friends during those six weeks: Wally
and Murdock.

Wally came from a Greek family and his last name was
Tsartsarlapidith, but our sergeant couldn't pronounce it
during our first roll call. He said, "Wally, somebody—
what the hell's your last name?"

"I forget, sir," Wally said.

Sergeant Krodecker was a tough professional soldier. He hollered, "DON'T CALL ME 'SIR'—I'M NOT A FUCKING OFFICER. All right, smart-ass, from now on your name is just WALLY."

Murdock was always just "Murdock"; I don't know why. He never used his first name. Not in front of us, anyway.

One day we were going through what they called the "Simulated Battlefield." We had to crawl under barbed wire, holding our rifles out in front of us, until we reached a grassy clearing. Murdock got through without trouble, and I followed him; but Wally, who was quite chubby, had a terrible time. Sergeant Krodecker hollered out, "WALLY, YOU'RE SLOWER THAN SHIT GOING THROUGH A TRUMPET!" I didn't like what he said, but I couldn't help laughing with all the others.

The next day I was on the firing range, which I was looking forward to. After I fired one shot with my rifle, it gave me a splitting headache and I thought I was going deaf. I also missed the target. I heard a voice behind me say, "What's your name, son?"

I turned and tried to see who was talking, but I had to look directly into the sun, and the man was just a silhouette. I couldn't really see his face except for a black, curly hair that looked like it was sticking out of his nose. I assumed he was an officer, so I said, "Pvt. Paul Peachy, sir."

"I'm Captain Harrington," the voice answered, "your company commander."

I started getting up as fast as I could, but he stopped me. "You don't have to get up," he said. "I just want you to try something for me. Before you fire your next round, take aim, take a small breath, hold it for a second . . . then *squeeze* the trigger, don't jerk it. Let me see you do that."

I did exactly what he said, and it worked. No bull's-eye, of course, but I hit the target. I was excited and I turned to him, but Captain Harrington was gone.

That night several of the boys in B Company began making up a song about Captain Harrington. They kept repeating it while they tried to find the harmony.

> *"Captain Harrington, as every soldier knows,*
> *has a curly black hair*
> *inside a wart upon his nose.*
>
> *"But 'Hair Nose Harrington' is really quite a sport.*
> *He never screams or yells,*
> *unless you stare right at his wart."*

Poor Captain Harrington. I hope he never hears it.

I'd never been on anything bigger than a rowboat before, but at 6:30 A.M. on May 7th, 1918, the Ninth Regiment sailed to France to fight the Huns.

Wally, Murdock, and I leaned over the ship's rail, watching New York disappear as the wind blew through our thoughts. I was wondering how Elsie reacted to my letter. Not that I regretted writing it—I just wondered if she was sad or relieved now that I was gone. I also wondered if I was going to die in France. I suppose all the fellows were thinking about that. I think that's why they told so many dumb jokes and made up stupid songs. We were all scared and didn't want to show it. I'm lucky I found Wally and Murdock. I would be so lonely without them.

THREE

⌒

WE LANDED AT SAINT-NAZAIRE, FRANCE, ON JUNE IST,
1918. It rained almost every day that first week, except
for one break in the weather that only lasted for an hour;
and we had to walk halfway to our destination when the
trucks couldn't get through the mud. I don't know what I
expected—a train ride I suppose.

We all wondered which little town we were being sent
to. I had a birthday coming up in a few days, and we
wondered if the French food would be as good as rumours said it was. When we arrived at our destination,

our little French town turned out to be miles and zigzag miles of muddy trenches, all lined with what they called "duckboards," which were wooden slats on the floor of the trenches. They were higher than the ground level so that soldiers could walk on the duckboards, over the water and mud.

Every soldier in the regiment was given three pairs of socks, to keep our feet dry, and we were told to change socks at least twice a day in order to prevent trench foot. We also had to rub our feet with whale-oil grease to stop water from getting to them. To top it off, the food wasn't any consolation.

On my thirtieth birthday, while we drank warm French beer and ate some soggy brioche, Wally and Murdock started singing "Happy Birthday" to me; but before they finished the song, Sergeant Krodecker ran in quickly, interrupting the last line.

"You speak German, Peachy?"

"Yes, Sergeant."

"Captain Harrington wants to see you. Now!" I grabbed my rifle and started running.

"AND DON'T LOOK AT HIS NOSE!" he hollered.

When I arrived in front of Captain Harrington, I saluted and then stayed at attention, stiff as a board. I tried to avoid staring at the black hair that curled out of the wart on his nose.

"Peachy, we're not formal in the rain and the mud—stand at ease!" he said. After I relaxed a little, he said, "Is it true you speak German?"

"Yes sir."

"Fluently?"

"Yes sir."

I think he began to notice that I never looked directly at him when I answered a question.

"You haven't done anything wrong, Peachy. Just relax. By the way, is 'Peachy' your real name or is that just a nickname?"

"Yes sir, it's my real name, but not my father's."

"What does that mean?"

"My father didn't speak English when he and my mother arrived from Germany. When Immigration asked for his name he kept repeating, 'Paquet,' but it sounded like 'Pachay' to them, so they wrote Peachy. Doesn't make sense, I know, sir, but that's what they did. His real name is Emil Paquet."

"Were you born in Germany?"

"No sir, Milwaukee, Wisconsin."

He let out half a laugh. "Where the beer comes from."

"Yes sir," I answered. I can't tell you how many times I've heard that joke.

"Well, I'm from Rhinelander, Wisconsin," he said. "Do you know it?"

"Oh sure, I mean, yes sir, I've heard of it. I always wanted to go fishing there someday."

"I hope you will—when this stinking war is over."

"I hope so, sir."

"The reason I sent for you is because a small reconnaissance just captured a German soldier who was wandering around in the woods about a quarter of a mile from here. I don't think he realised how close he was to his own side . . . or else he's lost his marbles. He won't speak to any of us—just keeps repeating, '*keine* English, *keine* English.' He was wearing a muddy corporal's uniform, but I believe he's an officer. I don't *know* that he's an officer—I just *think* he is. But keep my hunch in mind."

"Yes, sir."

"He's using the latrine now. I asked the two guards who captured him to take him to a dugout that has a few chairs and a cot. He looks starved, so bring him some coffee and a few sandwiches. We also have some cognac and some beer if he wants it." He smiled at me. "Not as good as Milwaukee beer, of course."

I faked another laugh.

"How much education have you had?"

"Through high school, sir, but I went to night school

after that. For two years."

"Studying what?"

"English and German literature, sir."

"Good for you. You have an honest face, Peachy, and the prisoner is exhausted—maybe he'll let his guard down if he talks German with someone. Any information you can get might be useful: Where did he come from? . . . Division? . . . Battalion? . . . Officers? . . . To what rank? . . . Tanks? . . . How many? Artillery support, cavalry . . . you understand what I mean?"

"Yes sir."

"They have at least one battalion two hundred yards straight in front of us, so how the hell did he get lost? Mostly we need to know what to expect if we attack. Clear?"

"Yes sir."

"I'm making you an acting corporal, Peachy. If you have any kind of trouble with him—get the hell out! I'll have someone stationed nearby. Clear?"

"Yes sir."

I saluted and sloshed my way back over the duckboards.

FOUR

WHEN I WALKED INTO THE DUGOUT AND SAW THE prisoner, two things struck me: that he had taken off his muddy corporal's uniform and was sitting on a chair in his underwear with his legs crossed—it was that his legs were crossed that struck me as odd. I wasn't sure why. The other thing was how calm he seemed, given the circumstances. The two guards who had captured him were standing nearby.

I placed the carton of food I had brought for the prisoner onto the table next to him, and then I dismissed the two guards. One of the guards, named Tom, called out to me before he left. "I'll be right outside. Just holler."

The prisoner was bigger than I expected—I mean taller, because he was very thin, with straight, golden blond hair. I would guess he was a little older than I was.

"Wie geht es Ihnen?" I asked. *("How are you?")* But he didn't even look at me, as if I should know it was a dumb question. When I asked if he would like some sandwiches, he exhaled a short, *"Ja,"* still without looking at me.

I sat down opposite him and watched as he ate two baloney and cheese sandwiches and drank a bottle of French beer.

While he ate I talked with him, in German, for almost half an hour. I tried sneaking in a trick question by saying that our cannons were so loud, they always gave me a terrible headache and did he have that problem? But no matter what I asked, he only gave me *"Ja's"* and *"Nein's."* I was feeling more and more foolish, when Tom, the guard, brought me my own supper. He set the tray down in front of me.

"Here ya go, pal," he said. "You ordered the coq au vin, didn't you?"

"That's right," I said.

"Lovely! Except that chef just ran out of coq au vin.

But he gave you some great imitation meatloaf—says it's even better than the chicken. Plus, he gave you a sort of cardboard cinnamon roll. Deelish! And here's a nice hot cup of two-day old mud. Chef swears by it."

"I'm sure he does. I'll be all right, Tom. You can go now."

Tom looked at the prisoner and said, "Call if you need me, Paul."

I tasted my food, but I wasn't hungry enough to brave eating much of it. After the prisoner finished his second sandwich I held up a bottle of brandy, which was only half full.

"Wünschen Sie noch einnen cognac?" I asked.

He looked at me with a funny smile. Then he said, in perfect English, "You have a funny accent, Paul."

I stared at him, like a mannequin. I realised that he had heard the guard call me Paul, but to suddenly speak English, after I had just talked to him for half an hour in German . . .

"Was one of your parents born in Germany?" he asked.

"Both of them," I said.

"May I ask where they came from? I don't recognise the region from the way you speak."

"They came from Flensburg," I answered.

"I've never heard of it," he said.

"It's near the Danish border," I said, like a good pupil.

"Ah! That explains it. Actually, I *would* like a little cognac, Paul. It's very kind of you, even if they did tell you to loosen me up."

How does he know everything? A corporal?

I filled a small glass of cognac, which he swallowed with one gulp. He sighed with satisfaction.

"That's better. Were you born in Germany, Paul?"

Are you just going to answer everything he asks, like some sort of dummy?

"No . . . America," I said, like a dummy.

"Where do you live in America?" he asked.

"You would never have heard of it."

"Try me," he said.

"It's in the Midwest—a town called Milwaukee," I said.

He started to laugh. "Where the beer comes from, yes?"

I nodded yes. He laughed again and said, "May I have a little more cognac, please?"

I poured him another small glass and then finally got the courage to speak.

"I don't understand—you said you didn't speak English."

"Was your father a schoolteacher?" he asked.

What would Captain Harrington want me to say?

"I'm not trying to trick you, Paul," he said. "I'm really just curious."

"My father was a baker."

"A baker! Oh, how nice for you. What was your favourite dessert?"

"Cremschnitten," I said.

He burst out laughing.

"Cremschnitten! Oh, my God—I haven't heard that word in a long time. My mother always made us say 'Napoleons.' I suppose it was a class thing."

Ask him. Now! Just ask him.

"Who are you?" I asked.

He looked straight at me for several seconds, then smiled.

"I'm a spy."

"For who?" I asked.

"For *whom?* Forgive me, Paul, that was cheap. For Germany. And for Britain, too—or so the British thought—but really only for Germany."

"May I ask how you got caught?" I asked.

"You shouldn't ask me if you 'may' ask me. Your company commander wouldn't like that. I didn't get caught, Paul—I wanted to be captured."

I was even more confused. "Why?" I asked.

"Because . . . *das lied ist aus,*" he said.

"I don't understand."

"My only contact in England sent me a short message, three days ago, which read: 'The song is over.'-"

"I don't understand anything that you're saying."

"Someone in British Intelligence found out who I am. I'm sure they've told the Americans by now . . . if not today, then tomorrow."

"Why didn't you stay in Germany?"

"Oh, it's over in Germany. We'll lose the war before the end of the year—they just don't know it yet. You can't imagine how stupid they are. And who knows what's going to happen in Germany after you win the war?"

"Are you changing sides?" I asked, hoping that I might get a real scoop to report to Captain Harrington.

"No, I'm not. Sorry to disappoint you, Paul," he said, probably because he noticed how much higher in pitch my voice had become.

"Why did you suddenly decide to speak to me in English?" I asked.

His eyes drifted away, as if I had asked him to explain a great mathematical problem. Then he looked at me. "Because I'm lonely. Could I have just one more cognac, Paul?"

I poured him another glass, finishing the bottle. Then I said, "May I ask what your name is?"

"I told you not to ask me if you 'may' ask me . . . we want to get you promoted one day, don't we?" he said with a gentle smile.

"Yes sir."

"My name? . . . Well, that depends. Before the war, my family owned several vineyards—only white wine, of course—you don't ever want to drink German red, Paul. But when the war started . . . because I was quite intelligent and spoke so many languages . . . I became a spy. My name used to be Franz von Teplitz."

"And now?"

"Now I'm an American. My name is Harry Stroller."

"Is that really true?" I asked.

"Well, not really, no—although my mother's name *was* Stroller and *she* was an American. You couldn't possibly believe how famous I am, Paul, for a person hardly anyone has met. Just a few generals and one colonel, that's all. Not even the Kaiser. No photos allowed. But *everyone in Germany* has heard of the great spy, Col. Harry Stroller."

"Are you German?"

"Yes, I am. My father was German, and he wouldn't have it any other way, despite my mother's feelings."

"Are you really a colonel?"

"Yes, I really am a colonel. I don't mean to be impolite, Paul—you've been very kind—but I'm very tired. Unless you have some Schubert you can play for me, do you mind if I sleep a little now?"

The prisoner lay down on the cot. Before he fell asleep, I needed to ask him one more question:

"What will happen if I tell them that you're a spy?"

"After they interrogate me?—They might wait until the war is over and then let me go . . . or they'll just shoot me."

"What should I do?" I asked.

"I don't care," he said, and fell asleep.

I stared at Harry Stroller, watching him snore by the light of the single candle that flickered nearby.

FIVE

⌒

JUST BEFORE THE SUN WAS ABOUT TO RISE, A NEW GUARD, who had taken Tom's place outside, rushed in and told me to grab some breakfast and report to Sergeant Krodecker as soon as possible. Two other soldiers came in and stood guard over the sleeping prisoner.

I still had a piece of roll in my mouth when I found Sergeant Krodecker. He said, "They tell me you're an acting corporal now, Peachy."

"Yes, Sergeant."

"Good for you. The Huns usually attack us early in the morning, but not until they've had their breakfast, of course—stuff yourself at breakfast then think about killing. But today we're going to attack first, and we don't want to run into any tear gas or mustard gas, so pick any two guys and take a look around out there. Don't go beyond the barbed wire—just look for gas clouds. Clear?"

"Yes, Sergeant."

My two pals were sitting nearby, sipping their coffee.

"Wally! Murdock! I'm supposed to take two men and go over the trench to see if there are any gas clouds around. Would you go with me?"

Murdock said, "Yes, sir, General." They both got up. We took our rifles, tightened our chin straps, and headed for the nearest fire steps, which we had to climb to get out of the trench. The sun was just starting to rise.

"We can't take more than a minute or two—we'll just go up to the first barbed wire," I shouted. When I saw that Murdock's feet were on the fire steps, I hollered, "Okay, GO!"

Murdock and Wally started climbing. I followed right behind them.

Two shots rang out. Wally and Murdock fell back into the trench. I turned and saw both of them lying face up on the floor of the trench, with their eyes open, staring at me. Both of them had a bullet through the head. I stood there looking at them—I don't know how long. A whistle shrieked and our whole company began climbing fire steps all along the trench, knocking me aside as they poured over the top and then ran toward the German trench. I climbed out of the trench and tried to keep up with the others, but I kept seeing the image of Wally and Murdock, surrounded by mud.

The German machine guns started firing and our soldiers began dropping like flies all around me. I saw a small woods to my right, maybe a quarter of a mile away. I turned and ran for the woods, stepping over dead and wounded soldiers. When I finally made it into the woods, I dropped to the earth, hugged a tree, and began to weep. I could hear rifles and machine guns in the distance.

After a few minutes, I got up and walked away from the sounds of battle and kneeled beside a nearby brook. I laid my rifle down and scooped some water onto my face. Then I took my helmet off and dropped my whole head into the cold water for fifteen or twenty seconds; then lifted my head and stared at the water, trying, but unable, to lessen the horrible realization that I was a coward. I was a coward, and there was no way to change that fact.

As I was about to rise, I saw a reflection in the water of a row of German soldiers standing behind me. I turned and saw a short but powerfully built German sergeant, who looked like a wrestler with a pig's head. He began shouting orders to the row of soldiers.

"Get this idiot on his feet," he yelled in German.

Two of his men pulled me up.

"This is the famous American soldier who has come to save the little Frenchmen? Put him up against a tree," Pig Head commanded.

The two soldiers grabbed my arms, dragged me away from the water, and shoved me against a tree.

"Because of you we are supposed to be afraid?" Pig Head shouted. "You are the mighty American soldier who is going to crush us? CLEAR OUT OF THE WAY!" he yelled to the soldiers next to me. They hurried back into formation. Then Pig Head yelled, "Ready . . ."

The seven soldiers raised their rifles.

"AIM . . ."

They pointed their rifles at my chest.

The curtain is up, Paul . . . the audience is waiting . . .

I don't know where it came from—I suddenly screamed, in German. "HALT! IDIOTS!—PUT DOWN YOUR RIFLES!"

Three or four of the soldiers were confused and lowered their rifles halfway. Pig Head went nearly crazy with rage.

"WHAT'S THE MATTER WITH ALL OF YOU?— SHOOT HIM!"

I started walking, quite calmly, toward the sergeant.

"You—Pig Head—come here," I said.

Now it was Pig Head who was confused. I shouted at him, "ASSHOLE! COME HERE, QUICKLY!"

Pig Head didn't know what to do. He started stuttering and sputtering. "But, but, what? But . . ."

"Give me your rifle!" I ordered.

The sergeant looked at the other solders, unsure of what he should do. I slapped him twice across the face. In reflex, he quickly handed me his rifle. I screamed at him, "Is this what you do when you capture an enemy soldier? No interrogation? Division? . . . Battalion? . . . Company? . . . Officers? . . . To what rank? Tanks? How many? Artillery support? Cavalry? Is this what we've been teaching you? To capture a prisoner and shoot him, without one word coming out of HIS mouth? You are a disgrace to Germany!"

The sergeant was dumbfounded. His mouth hung open, but nothing came out.

I turned to one of the other soldiers. "You, Corporal!— You're in command. Now take me to your company commander, and for Christ's sake—LET ME SEE A GERMAN SOLDIER!"

After the corporal gave a command, I walked beside them as they all marched away, with Pig Head trailing behind, bewildered.

SIX

~

THIRTY MINUTES LATER I WAS WAITING IN THE HALLWAY of a small castle. The company commander I was waiting to see couldn't have been a very important officer because this castle seemed to be falling apart. The walls were gray with dirt, and there were tiny stone particles on the floors. A corporal had given me a stein of beer while I waited, which I much appreciated; but after only a few minutes he said, "Captain Simmel is ready for you now, sir."

Capt. Stefan Simmel was a short, ridiculous-looking

man with a great capacity for nervousness, which I could see he was trying to hide under an exterior of great confidence; but his sweat gave him away. He was sitting behind his desk as he watched me approach. From the stupid grin on his face, I'm sure he thought I was an imposter. But he probably had to make sure.

"So . . . I have the honour of actually being in the same room with the great Harry Stroller. It takes my breath away," he said. "Please sit, *Mister Stroller*," he said, pointing to the chair opposite him.

"I'm not *Mister* Stroller—I'm *Colonel* Stroller," I answered, and sat down.

Simmel walked around his desk and stood in front of me. I stayed seated. We were two or three feet apart.

"How are you today . . . *Mister* Stroller?"

I stared at him for a second, then rose from my chair and threw all of my beer into his face. Simmel was drenched as the beer dripped down onto his immaculate uniform.

"How . . . how . . . are you today, *Colonel* Stroller?" he stammered. "I hope you are well, I hope."

"Wonderful! How are you?" I asked.

"Wonderful! I'm wonderful," he answered.

The phone rang and Simmel tried to wipe his face and pat his uniform with a handkerchief as he answered.

"Hullo . . . Oh, yes sir, this is Captain Simmel speaking. Yes sir . . . he's here now, right in front of me. Yes . . . Colonel Stroller! . . . that's what he said, sir. One moment, please . . ."

Simmel turned to me. "Col. Viktor Steinig wants to know why all of this is not going through code channels."

"Tell him . . . because . . . the song is over."

"What, sir? I'm sorry, but what are you saying?"

"Someone in British Intelligence knows who Harry Stroller is. The Americans probably know by now—if not today than tomorrow. All contacts must be informed immediately."

Simmel repeated the information almost mechanically. As he listened to Colonel Steinig's response, he became even more shaken. "Yes sir, I understand. I'll tell him immediately. Thank you, sir."

Simmel hung up with a contorted smile on his face. "Colonel Steinig welcomes you, sir. An auto will take you to him as soon as you are ready. He begs you—and I beg you, too, sir—to just relax and refresh yourself, and perhaps you would care to bathe and put on a fresh *German* uniform?" he said, with an apologetic smile. "It's more than an hour's journey to his headquarters."

"Thank you," I answered.

"There is a guest room upstairs, sir . . . my orderly will take you there. I think you will find everything you need." Then he shouted, *"Korporal!"*

The corporal ran in and stood at attention as Simmel gave him instructions.

"The guard will show you the way. Is there anything else I can get for you, *Colonel* Stroller?"

"Another beer would be nice," I said, and handed him my empty beer stein.

Forty-five minutes later I walked out of Colonel Simmel's *schloss* wearing a colonel's uniform, which was a size too small for me, and a beautiful hat, which was a size too big for me. I stuffed my muddy private's uniform into some wrapping paper that I had requested. I didn't want to give Simmel anything he could use if he decided to do a check on me. I put the package under my arm and walked out.

A beautiful automobile was waiting for me. The back-seat door was already open, and an elderly driver in a corporal's uniform came to attention as I approached. He gave me a pleasant smile and saluted. I resisted my instinctive American salute and imitated his. Then we drove off.

I sat in silence for ten or fifteen minutes, trying to

overcome the increasing panic I was feeling about what would happen to me when we arrived. I wanted to talk to someone.

"This is a swell car," I said, without thinking.

The driver turned his head. "Pardon me, sir?"

"What a beautiful machine this is," I said, recovering my senses. "Is it new?"

"No sir, it's a nineteen twelve Mercedes. But we try to keep it looking like new."

I could see, in his rear-view mirror, that he was pleased with my comment. I supposed the "we" meant that he took care of the car himself and was proud of the way it looked. He seemed a little old to be only a corporal, with his bright silver sideburns disappearing into his hat, but he was a pleasant man and after a few more minutes I said, "May I ask your name?"

"Tausk, sir," he answered. "Cpl. Joseph Tausk."

"I'm glad to meet you, Corporal Tausk."

"Thank you, sir," he said, slightly surprised, I think, that a colonel would deign to talk to him and even break the normal social barrier.

More silence. I looked out of the window at the beautiful countryside we were passing, but I soon started thinking about Murdock and Wally, lying in the trench with their eyes open. *How long can I keep this up? How could I have screamed at all those German soldiers and slapped their sergeant in the face? . . . and thrown beer in that stupid Captain Simmel's face? I don't have the nerve to do things like that . . . I don't . . . and yet I did.*

SEVEN

WHEN WE ARRIVED AT COLONEL STEINIG'S MAGNIFICENT
castle I was overwhelmed: tall poplar trees, with wild
flowers in bloom all across the lawns, and a small lake on
one side of the castle with two swans floating in it.

As we drove up, Joseph Tausk opened the door of the
Mercedes, and I stepped out, almost tripping over the
polished boots I'd been given. Two guards and an officer
were waiting. The officer saluted and said, "An honour,
sir. Please follow me." I followed him into the castle.

We went through an immense baronial hall, up a flight of stairs that looked like they were made of marble, then down a long corridor with an open door at the end. As I got closer to the open door I felt like—I don't remember the expression, "A bull in a china shop?" or, "A pig in a bun shop?"—I just know that I felt ridiculous in this stupid, tight uniform I was wearing and the polished boots and the big hat. I took off the hat.

The officer ushered me into the study and there sat Col. Viktor Steinig, mid forties, sitting behind a highly polished mahogany desk. He was extremely handsome, with a full head of silver-and-blond hair, combed back so that his forehead was prominent. He had piercing blue eyes; and judging from the smooth skin on his unwrinkled face, I would bet that he got a massage every day.

As he saw me enter, he got up quickly, nodded to the officer, who left the room immediately, and then walked toward me with a warm smile. We shook hands.

"Harry!" he said.

"Viktor!" I answered.

He was either being very polite, or he was trying to put me off guard. After we shook hands, he never took those piercing blue eyes off me. Not for a moment. I had the feeling he was waiting for me to make some tiny slip. After staring at me for what seemed like ten or fifteen seconds, he said, *"Deutsch oder Englisch?"*

"You speak English?"

"Perfectly," he answered.

"Oh well, it doesn't matter," I said, wondering which choice was the trap. Then I said, *"Deutsch!"*

"I prefer that we speak in English. Do you mind?"

"Not at all," I answered. *Then why ask me? I suppose he just wanted to know which language I would choose.*

"So, we meet at last," he said. "You can't know how pleased I am."

"Thank you."

"You know, Harry, you're shorter than I thought you would be," he said, with a quizzical smile.

"Well, actually, Viktor—you're a little taller than I imagined *you* would be. I also thought you would be bald—don't ask me why. Funny the way we draw pictures in our minds."

"You seem uncomfortable, Harry. Are you a little nervous?"

"You would be uncomfortable, too, if you had to wear this ridiculously tight uniform."

"Of course, of course—Please forgive me. I'll send my tailor to your room whenever you're ready. Tell me—does duty permit you to rest for a little while or must you rush off somewhere and be brilliant?"

"To tell you the truth, Viktor—I'm exhausted . . . and a little lonely. I've been through so much recently. Actually, my superiors insisted that I relax for a while."

"Wonderful! Stay here and rest for a week or two. I'm sure you deserve a vacation. May I offer you some wine?"

"That would be nice. Thank you."

"White or red, Harry?

Trap . . . Stroller said, "You don't ever want to drink German red, Paul."

"Some white would be wonderful," I answered.

"I'll have some cold Champagne sent to your room, Harry. Do you mind if I ask where you learned to speak English?"

"At home."

"From who?" he asked.

"From *whom*," I answered. "I'm sorry—that was cheap. From my mother. She was American."

Good . . . Harry Stroller, you came through for me.

"Oh, of course, I remember now. Harry, why don't you take a little nap before dinner? I'm giving a small party tonight, just a few friends . . . I'd love you to come. A little music and dancing and some delicious food . . . it will do you good."

"Well . . ."

"I insist," Steinig said, being very positive but very

charming as well.

Stroller would probably enjoy it. "Thank you. I'd be delighted," I said.

"Good for you." Steinig took both my hands. "Harry, I hope we can become friends." He shook my hand. "Go and get some rest now."

I couldn't tell whether this was all an act on his part or if he actually meant it.

A servant showed me into a luxurious bedroom. I'd never seen the likes of it—not even in any of the magazines that travellers left behind on my train. It had an enormous bed and a ceiling so high you would need a ladder to reach it. There was a silver bucket on the table next to the bed, with two glasses on a tray. The bucket was filled with ice and it held a bottle of already opened Champagne. There was also a bowl of fruit next to it. And only a few hours ago, I was running for my life.

"Would you care for a glass of Champagne, sir? the servant asked.

"Thank you, I would."

The servant poured a glass of bubbles, which soon calmed down. "Sir—" he said, offering it to me. He waited to see if I liked it.

"Delicious!" I said.

How would I know if it was delicious? This was only the second time in my life that I'd drunk Champagne. The first time was when Elsie and I got married.

The servant said, "Thank you, sir," and left.

I wandered around the room, sipping Champagne, feeling wonderful and ridiculous at the same time. It's true what I heard about the bubbles tickling your nose. I had to keep remembering not to take too big a sip.

I took off my boots and walked over to the open window in the centre of the room, which had mouldings of miniature naked men and women all around it. They looked like they had been hand carved. Soft, blue velvet drapes hung on each side of the window, just touching the naked figures. I would never have seen this in Milwaukee—not if I lived to be a hundred. But because I was a coward who ran away when the machine guns started killing everyone around me, I'm given a room to live in that looks as close to Heaven as I'll ever get.

I was curious to see the bathroom. I wasn't disappointed. It was gigantic, with two large sinks and a bathtub that you could almost swim in, with enough towels for a family of four.

On my way out of the bathroom, I took a handful of grapes and walked over to the open window. It was a beautiful day. The June air felt so clean as it blew across my face. I looked out over four or five acres of lawn. There were deer grazing at the far end, just below an apple tree.

Directly below me was a cobblestone walk, with a small garden behind it. I dropped one of my grapes and watched it fall . . . it seemed to take forever before it landed. Too far for me to jump I told myself. And if I did jump and if I didn't break my bones—where would I go?

After relieving myself in the bathroom, I walked to the large bed, pulled back the comforter, and lay down on pillows so soft that my head must have sunk six inches. On the ceiling above me there was a painting of four angels, playing together. They each had tiny wings. I couldn't tell which were girl angels and which were little boys, but they were all smiling and having fun. I envied them.

This had been the strangest day of my life. The Champagne was getting to me. After a few minutes I fell asleep and dreamed that Murdock and Wally were still lying in the trench, with their eyes open, but they were smiling at me. And just as Wally was about to say something that I desperately wanted to hear . . . I woke up. Then I soaked in the beautiful hot water in my enormous private bathtub.

EIGHT

⌒

AN HOUR AND A HALF LATER I WAS DRESSED IN A NAVY
blue suit, white shirt, and light blue tie, standing in front
of the full-length mirror in my room. A short, Italian
tailor, with dark hair and a glamorous moustache, was
standing beside me, admiring his work.

"So—you like?" he asked.

"You're a wonderful tailor," I said. "I don't know how
you did it."

"No, is simple. I have a nice blue suit from a general

before he goes to make the war . . . I make a few snips, I cut some shoulders, I fix the sleeves . . . and is perfect. He leaves you nice shoes, too, yes?"

"Yes, they fit very well. You're a genius."

"Yes, I am a genius. You need something else?" he asked.

"Nothing. Thank you."

The tailor made a little bow and left the room.

Music from a string quartet drifted up to my room through the open window. I took one last look at myself in the mirror, took a deep breath for courage, and walked down the marble stairway, following the Strauss waltz.

I walked into a small ballroom and saw fifteen or twenty guests, mingling in little groups. Most of the men were officers—nothing lower than a captain—and the women were dressed formally, in white, mostly. A few couples were dancing. At one end of the room there were several tables overflowing with meats and pastries. Servants were pouring Champagne.

I heard a voice calling out, "HARRY!" and turned to see Colonel Steinig beckoning me to come over to his little group.

When I arrived, he said, "Harry, I would like to introduce you to some dear friends of mine who are most anxious to meet you. It gives me great pleasure to introduce Count von Oppersdorf. Count, may I present our former liaison to Briton—Col. Harry Stroller.

I shook hands with the Count, who was actually in his general's uniform, and said, "It's a pleasure, sir." Then Steinig said, "Any may I present the Countess von Oppersdorf.

The Countess was a heavyset woman with an adorable smile. She was quite shy and giddy with anticipation as she offered me her hand. I shook hands with her. Steinig looked horrified, but the Countess burst out laughing. Then the Count began to laugh.

The Countess said, "Colonel Stroller, this is the first time somebody makes me laugh for so long. Thank you."

I could see that Steinig was very relieved. He said, "Instead of kissing her hand, Harry shakes it, like an American cowboy. What would you have done, General, if an ordinary person had just done that to your wife?"

"I would have shot him," he said, and they all laughed so loudly that tears came to the Countess's eyes.

"That was refreshing, Harry," the Count said. "You will forgive my wife—she is too embarrassed to practice her English in public."

"There's no need," I said.

"No, but I want her to learn. It may become important,

soon. What can I do to help her get over this shyness?"

"Take her shopping in London," I said.

They all burst out laughing again. "Young man," the Count said, "I'm glad that you are on our side. And now, I think I will have a little dance with my wife."

I shook the Count's hand. The Countess offered me her hand again and this time I kissed it. As they moved off, Steinig moved close to me.

"Harry, you are the hit of the party," he said. Then he moved very close to me and whispered, "And now, my friend, for some serious business: Would you like a woman?"

Does he really mean what it sounds like? It's probably better if he thinks I'm a joker instead of an idiot.

"To tell you the truth, Viktor, I think I'd rather have one of those pastries over there."

"No, no! No more games, Harry," he continued in a whisper. "Tell me the truth—I'm your friend—would you like to be with a woman tonight?"

I felt like a fool. I didn't know what to answer.

"Forgive me, Harry," Steinig said, "I would not exactly win a prize for tact. Of course you would. It's probably been a long time for you. May I make the selection? I've lived with your reputation for so long that I think I know even your taste in women." He looked across the room, searching for someone. "Her name is Annie Breton, and she is standing . . . there!"

He pointed to a small brunette, quite thin, who was wearing a red-and-black gown that seemed out of place somehow next to all of the elegant gowns around her. She looked to be about twenty-seven or twenty-eight. I couldn't tell if she was pretty because she was wearing so much make-up that it made her look cheap, but her small body was attractive. She was talking with a young officer.

"Annie is French, Harry. She has great class . . . and she's a pig. That's a nice combination, don't you think? If you're disappointed, tell me tomorrow and you can pick any bottle you like from my cellar."

"But she's with someone," I said, hoping for relief.

"Oh, pooh! He's a captain; you're a colonel. She'll like you more. You go over and get something to eat while I make the arrangements. Try some of those Napoleons— they're delicious."

As Steinig walked away I went directly to the pastry table and looked at all the beautiful cakes and tortes and, of course, the *Cremschnitten*. I picked one up and took a bite . . . it was delicious. Much more delicate than the "Napoleons" we had in Milwaukee.

"Colonel Stroller?"

I was so absorbed with my *Cremschnitten* that I didn't realise someone was talking to me.

"Harry Stroller?" the voice repeated. I turned to see that it was the little brunette with all the make-up who was talking to me. She was smiling.

"Don't you know your own name?" she asked. She spoke in English with a slight French accent.

"I'm sorry . . . I forget sometimes."

"Maybe you should tie a string around your finger," she said.

"What if I forget to look at my finger?"

"Would you like me to stand next to you all the time, just in case?" she asked.

"It might look a little funny."

"Then why don't we dance?" she said. "That way, no one will notice."

She had a sense of humour—thank goodness. I smiled, wiped the whipped cream off my face and hands, and led her into the waltz that the string quartet was playing. My mother had taught me how to dance the waltz, so I was comfortable, at least for now.

As we danced, I caught Colonel Steinig's eye. He smiled and nodded a sign of approval. That was how I met Annie Breton.

NINE

⌒

WE LEFT THE PARTY EARLY AND I WENT WITH ANNIE
to her apartment. I had never done anything like this
before, but I was afraid of what Viktor might think of
Harry Stroller if he didn't follow through with his arr-
angement. That's only partly true . . . I have to confess
that I was also aroused by the idea. I hadn't been with a
woman for such a long time. The last time was with my
wife, six months ago.

As we entered Annie's living room, we were met by a

maid. Annie handed her evening wrap to the maid but never spoke to her and, apart from "Good evening" to me, the maid never said another word. She seemed to have a routine where she knew exactly what was to be done at each moment. The maid and I followed Annie into her bedroom.

When I saw the bed I became very nervous. It was a four poster, with canopy, and there was a small table at the foot of the bed with an ice bucket and a bottle of Champagne, already opened.

"Help yourself to Champagne," Annie said, pointing to the bottle. "Maria will take your jacket." Maria took my jacket and hung it over a man's valet stand, which suddenly lessened any erotic thoughts I had.

As the maid lowered the light from the gas lamps, I heard Annie, in her bathroom, calling out, "I hope you don't like a lot of light." It was as if she could see through the walls at what the maid was doing.

"Do you want me to call you Colonel or Colonel Stroller or Herr Stroller or Herr Harry or what name would you prefer?" Annie called out.

I almost said, "Just call me Paul," but I caught myself in time. "Just call me Harry," I said.

"Oh, good. If you'd like to undress now, Maria will hang up your things."

The maid waited for me to hand her my "things." I just shook my head no. Maria moved to the phonograph, which was near the head of the bed. I wondered if Annie had also timed the music. Then I heard her call from the bathroom, "Do you like music, Harry?"

"Yes," I answered.

A romantic French song began to play as Maria put the needle onto the phonograph record that was already in place. Then she turned down the bed and left the room. After a few moments, Annie came out, dressed—or I should say, almost undressed—in a very sheer lavender negligee.

"Would you pour us some Champagne, Harry?" I was more than a little nervous as I poured two glasses of Champagne. Annie took off her negligee, exposing her bare bosom. She had small breasts, which relieved me somehow. I know it sounds silly, but I always found small breasts more erotic whenever I saw young women talking together on the train, even though they were fully clothed. I told my "small breast theory" to Murdock once, when he was eating lunch, and he laughed so hard he nearly choked.

Annie sat at the edge of her bed and crossed her legs, wearing only her white panties. I'd say it was a sexy pose except for all of her garish make-up, which dampened my sexual impulses. It made her look like the whores I used to see walking on Fondulac Avenue in Milwaukee, with their lips covered with so much lipstick that you couldn't tell what they really looked like, and with blue eyelids, fake rosy cheeks, and eyelashes loaded with mascara. Annie's naked body was very small and I think attractive, but her nakedness made her make-up seem that much uglier to me. The strong perfume she must have just doused herself with in the bathroom made me feel slightly ill. I had a strong inclination to just walk out. And yet . . .

"What shall we drink to, Monsieur Harry?" she asked.

"The Kaiser," I said, stalling for time.

"Oh, you—let's drink to us!"

We clicked glasses and I took a sip of Champagne. Then she stood up and kissed me tenderly, on both cheeks, as her tiny breasts pressed lightly against my shirt. She slipped off her panties and sat back down on the bed. Elsie was the only other woman I had ever seen completely naked, and then only after she turned the lamps way down.

"Harry, I don't know if you're trying to look at me or trying not to look at me," she said, half smiling but with a puzzled look.

"Both," I said.

"Why don't you come closer and let me help you off with your clothes?"

I stood still, looking at her beautiful body. It was so smooth it reminded me of the alabaster figurines I used to see at the museum in Milwaukee.

"Don't you want to make love with me?" she asked, almost like a little girl.

"Yes, I do."

"It's not that you like boys, is it?" she asked, suddenly quite serious.

"No, nothing like that. Would you take your make-up off?" I asked.

She seemed a little startled.

"Why?" she asked.

"So I can see your face."

"I'd rather not," she said. "My face is very ordinary. Anyway, what's wrong with my face the way it is? No one has ever complained."

"It makes you look like a whore," I said, regretting how terrible it sounded when it came out of my mouth, but that's how I felt.

Annie covered her body with a blanket and said, "Would you get out, please?"

"I'm sorry if I hurt you."

"Please get out, Colonel."

I took my jacket off of the valet stand and left.

When I stepped outside I saw Joseph and the car waiting for me. The air was cold for a June night, but I was burning. I knew I had hurt her feelings, but I had told the truth—she did look like a whore, and the look of her and the smell of her perfume *did* make me sick. But there was more to it than just my great, manly honesty . . . I was also afraid to make love to Annie because I kept thinking of Elsie.

That night I dreamt that I was sitting naked on a bed, with my legs crossed, feeling very embarrassed. I was staring at some person, or persons, and I heard one of them call out, in an orderly, very calm manner: "Ready . . . Aim . . ." but before he could say "Fire" I heard a loud knocking, which woke me up.

TEN

~

"COME IN," I TRIED TO CALL OUT WITH MY SQUEAKY
voice. A servant walked in and said, "Please, excuse me,
sir—I'm so sorry—it was an order from Colonel Steinig."
Then he placed a tray of biscuits, cheese, jam, and a pot
of hot coffee beside my bed.

Another servant came in with a beautiful field gray
military uniform and hat, which he said came from the
tailor. The collar and cuffs were piped in white. Then
he laid a pair of white gloves beside the uniform, on the

chaise longue, along with a Lugar pistol, with holster and belt. It was difficult for me to imagine myself walking out in public wearing all of this. He explained that Colonel Steinig hoped that I would go with him to inspect the young recruits who had drilled so well during their first week of training.

After breakfast, I put on my new dress uniform, with my Lugar pistol, white gloves, and hat. I felt like I was going to perform in an operetta. I had worn a pistol once before, in a play at the Milwaukee Players, but that pistol was made of painted clay. What in the world would I do with a real pistol—shoot my way out of Germany?

Joseph was standing next to his Mercedes. I nodded to him and he smiled. Viktor and I got into the Mercedes, and Joseph drove us to the parade grounds. As we approached, we saw columns of soldiers standing at ease. They all jumped to attention when their company commander hollered out an order. His face reminded me of one of those villains in the silent movies I used to see in Milwaukee.

When we got out of the Mercedes, Steinig said, "You're something of a folk hero to them, Harry. This band of Boy Scouts comes from the last pickings of our reserves—useless, of course, but they'll make good guinea pigs—if they don't shoot us by mistake. I hope you don't mind that I accepted for you."

"Well . . . only that I haven't done this for such a long time, Viktor."

"Oh, poof! Just walk through and swear at one or two of them—they'll love that."

I walked slowly between three rows of soldiers, followed closely by the ugly company commander. Steinig stayed behind, watching, with a smile on his face.

All the young men were stiff as boards, so nervous that their eyes were popping. I looked at their shoes, ties, and belt buckles, trying to act like an officer. Mostly I was remembering Annie, with her small breasts pressing against my shirt as she kissed my cheek on both sides.

I noticed an unbuttoned shirt on one of the young soldiers. "You missed a button on your shirt," I said, and then turned quickly to see if the company commander had noticed; he obviously had because his face was turning red.

"What's your name?" I asked the boy.

"Kluck, sir," he said, trying to answer without crying.

"Where are you from?"

"Stuttgart, sir."

Then he started to cry. It was too late for me to save

him. "Stop crying. Don't cry," I said. "I'm going to swear at you. When I'm done, stand up straight and say, 'Yes sir,' and give me a smart salute. I began swearing, using the few German swear words that I remembered. I pointed to his shirt and yelled, "What in Christ's name is this supposed to be . . . the latest style in Stuttgart?" He looked down for a moment and I screamed, "Keep your head up, imbecile, and don't ever let this happen again," which sounded ridiculous as soon as I said it, but the boy stopped crying and gave me a nice salute, holding back a smile.

As I continued down the aisle, I came to a smug-looking soldier with bulging muscles, who couldn't seem to hold back a cocky smile. He reminded me of my Basic Training days in Arkansas, when some big brute, who thought he was King of the Mountain, would pound the arms of the youngest recruits until they were black and blue if they didn't pay him proper respect. Still, I knew that I shouldn't jump to conclusions just because of a cocky smile. I stopped in front of him and asked for his name.

"I am Pvt. Conrad Hoffman, sir," he answered, in a superior tone.

"Are you a good soldier?" I asked.

"I am the best soldier in this platoon, sir," he answered.

I looked him in the eye. His grin grew bigger. "And do

you beat up the smaller boys who don't pay you proper respect?" I asked.

At first my question caught him off guard; then I think he took it as a compliment and said, "Only when they misbehave, sir."

I brushed the fingers of one of my white gloves across the muzzle of his rifle—they remained immaculately clean. The cocky soldier's smile grew bigger. I looked at the commanding officer, who was standing a short distance away, watching us intently. I looked at my glove and shook my head in disgust, as if my glove was filthy. Then I walked away. The smile disappeared from the cocky recruit's face.

An absurdly young boy was next in line.

"How old are you?" I asked.

"Almost seventeen, sir," he answered, in a high-pitched voice, as if it had only just changed from soprano to squeaky alto. I wanted to give him a hug and send him home.

"Do you write to your mama?" I asked.

"Yes sir," he answered.

"What do you do in civilian life?" I asked.

"I'm a baker's assistant to my father, sir."

"Really?" I said. "My father was a baker. Do you and your father make *cremschnitten?*"

"Oh, yes sir," he said, with a big smile.

"Don't smile! You'll get us both in trouble. Did you enlist in the army?" I asked.

"Yes sir," he answered.

"That was dumb," I said, and moved on.

When I finally finished this ridiculous routine, I walked back to Steinig. "Excellent," he said. "They were thrilled."

As we walked to the Mercedes, he said, "Harry, if you're not going to tell me, I am most certainly going to ask. How was Annie?"

"You can keep your wine cellar intact," I answered, trying to conceal my real feelings.

Steinig laughed. "I knew it. There are very few sure bets in life, but that was one of them. Would you like to see her again?" he asked.

"Are you the local matchmaker, Viktor?"

He laughed again. "Only for special guests. The reason I ask is because I'm giving a very small dinner tonight for a family that has been so kind to me. It will only be these dear friends . . . but I can ask Annie, if you like."

"To tell you the truth . . . I don't think she would come."

"Nonsense—I know she would. I'd be happy to ask her, but only if you like."

After a pause, I said, "Yes, I would like."

"Good! Then I'll invite her."

ELEVEN

THAT NIGHT THERE WERE SEVEN OF US SITTING AROUND a small, very elegant dinner table: Gen. Max von Baden— in whose honour this dinner was being given—his wife, Marianne, and their two children who were in their late teens. Steinig sat at one end of the table, me at the other, and Annie in the middle.

Annie wore a black evening dress, which matched well with the men's tuxedos, but her "whore's" make-up looked about the same as the last time I saw her. Perhaps a *little* lighter.

After quails eggs, caviar, venison, Napoleons, and three glasses of wine (white), everyone at the table—except Annie—wanted to know what I used to do when I lived in America with my mother. I stupidly blabbered that I had once acted on the stage. Well, you would think that Rudolph Valentino had just walked in. Steinig urged me to recite something from one of the plays and everyone joined in, begging me to perform—everyone except Annie. I finally stood up, wishing I had kept my big mouth shut, and tried not to show how tipsy I was. I began reciting a speech from Shakespeare's *Julius Caesar*—one of the plays I was in at the Milwaukee Players. I was hoping I could still remember the lines:

> "There is tears for his love;
> joy, for his fortune;
> honour, for his valour . . . and . . ."

What the hell's the next line? I shouldn't have had so much wine. Take a long pause, they'll think you're acting . . . Wait, I remember . . .

> ". . . and *death,* for his ambition."

I looked slowly at each one of the guests as they watched me.

"Who is here so base, that would be a bondman?
If any, speak; for him have I offended.

Who is here so rude, that would not be a Roman?
If any, speak; for him have I offended."

Start getting emotional . . .

"Who is here so vile, that will not love his country?
If any, speak; for HIM have I offended. I pause for
a reply."

I lowered my head, dramatically, as any good ham actor would do. The guests, led by Colonel Steinig, burst
into applause. I looked at Annie to see if I had made any
impression on her, but all I saw was confusion in her eyes.
I downed the remainder of my fourth glass of wine.

Steinig said, "Harry, this was out of this world."

Madame von Baden said, "But where did you learn
this? . . . I mean, this is the work of a professional actor."

"You're too kind, Madame," I said, trying to respond as
Barrymore would.

The general said, "Is there yet another secret that we don't know, Harry? Were you actually famous in America?"

"No, no," I said. "Honestly. Oh, at one time I had ambitions—I appeared on Broadway a few times, but—"

Ilse, the von Baden's daughter, nearly went wild. She practically screamed, "BROADWAY?"

"Yes," I said, "but that was a long time ago, Ilse, when I lived in New York with my mother. You mustn't make too much of it."

The general said, "It seems to me that a Broadway actor in the German army should at least be a general."

Everyone laughed and applauded. I looked at Annie. She was staring at me, but she wasn't laughing or applauding. Karl von Baden, their son, asked, "Who did you act with on Broadway, Colonel Stroller? Would we know any of them by name?"

"I don't think you would have heard of them, Karl," I answered. "I hardly remember them myself."

Ilse said, "Oh please, Colonel Stroller—try to remember. I used to dream of going to New York and seeing the Broadway musicals."

"Well—I think there was a Fred somebody . . . No, not Fred . . . George! George Cohan."

Ilse cried out, "GEORGE M. COHAN? MAMA, DID

YOU HEAR THAT?"

Madame von Baden almost rose out of her seat. "Max—he knows George M. Cohan!"

The general said, "Now this is too much, Harry. Tell us honestly . . . don't you ever wish you were back on the stage?"

I thought I had better put some water on the fire I had lit before it got out of hand. "Never," I said. "I have more important things to do than play little games."

Annie had a quizzical smile on her face. "You seem to be very good at playing little games, Colonel Stroller." There was a tense pause. Sensing it, Steinig quickly jumped in:

"Annie," he said, "can you picture Harry having lunch with the prime minister of England, sitting between Lloyd George and General Allenby?—and while offering Harry a cigar, Allenby asks him, 'Where do *you* think we should strike next?'-"

"Is this really true, Harry?" General von Baden asked. "He really asked you that?"

"Yes, yes, that's how I remember it," I said.

"And what did you answer?" Annie asked.

"Well, I puffed on his cigar and stammered and stalled for as long I could—my mind racing a mile a minute—but no matter what I thought of, I ended up red in the face."

Annie said, "But why, Colonel Stroller?—you seem

always to know the right thing to say."

"Yes, but I don't smoke cigars," I answered.

Everyone let out a huge laugh—except Annie. "I see it's very difficult to know when you're telling the truth, Colonel Stroller."

Steinig quickly saved me again. "Why do you think they made him a spy, Annie? That's where the genius comes in."

General von Baden rose from the table and said, "Well I would like to ask you a question, Colonel Stroller. I am a general and I order you to tell me the truth: To the best of your knowledge, when do you predict that this war will be over?"

Steinig leaned forward ever so slightly.

I took a long pause, as if I were trying to decide how much information I could share, and then I said, "From the best source of information I have, Herr General . . . I would say that the war will be over . . . by Christmas."

The general was ecstatic. "*Phantastisch!* That is exactly when my staff has predicted: next Christmas."

"No! *This* Christmas," I said.

Steinig was stunned. The general was flabbergasted. Looking me sternly in the eye, the general said, "Young man, are you seriously telling me that we will win the war by Christmas of 1918?"

"I'm saying . . . that . . . yes, we will win the war by Christmas of 1918."

The general sat down, but his mouth remained open with disbelief. "You're either crazy or a genius," he said.

Karl, the son, rose and said, "I propose a toast: to Christmas—1918!"

They all raised their glasses: "TO CHRISTMAS—1918!"

When the dinner party was over and I had said my good-byes to all the other guests, I walked up to Annie.

"Good night, Mademoiselle Breton."

"*Oh, la la!* We are suddenly the perfect gentleman tonight—aren't we, Herr Colonel? Could such an important actor as yourself possibly spare the time to walk me to my auto?"

We walked out of the castle and onto the driveway. It was a beautiful night, a little chilly, but with a clear sky. I walked Annie to her auto. "You don't have a driver?" I asked.

"I'm not as wealthy as you are, Colonel Stroller," she said. Then she stood very still and looked at my eyes for several seconds, as if she were trying to see past my words. "Would you like to come to my apartment, Harry?" she asked.

"I'm . . . a little tired . . . and a little drunk, Annie. But thank you."

She stared at me, trying to decide, I think, whether I was telling the truth or just putting her off.

"Well then—would you like to kiss me good night?" she asked.

After a pause I said, "No."

"Why?"

"Because you have so much make-up on, I might miss your lips."

She looked at me for a few seconds and then slapped me so hard across the face that I felt my drunken head start to twirl. She got into her auto and drove off.

TWELVE

⌒

THE NEXT MORNING I RECEIVED A HAND-DELIVERED
message.

Dear Monsieur Harry:

*I was very angry last night. I thought I was angry
with you, but I realised later that I was angry
with myself. I owe some kind of explanation for
my behaviour. It may change your opinion of me.*

Perhaps not. If you don't want to see me again, that's all right. If you do, please call.

Kind regards,
Annie
01-24-30-71

"Hullo . . ."

I wasn't sure if it was Annie or her maid.

"Annie?" I asked.

"Yes."

"This is Monsieur Harry. You remember me, don't you?"

"Yes, I remember you very well."

"I would like to meet with you someplace, now that I'm not drunk. But not at your apartment, if that's all right."

She paused for a moment and then said, "There is a Japanese garden not too far from where I live. It's called Karlsruhe Japanese Garden. It's also called Stadtgarten."

"You're sure I'll be able to find it?"

"Oh, yes. Anyway, your driver will know it. You enter through a red gate and at the far end of the garden you'll find a Shinto shrine that's guarded by two very large, stone Lion Dogs—I promise you won't miss them. Follow the small footpath, which will lead you to my favourite place,

next to a young maple tree. We can sit and talk there. It's
very peaceful."

"What time?"

"In an hour—if that's all right?"

"I'll see you there in an hour."

The two Lion Dogs were easy to find. I suppose they were
meant to scare off any people who would harm the Shinto
shrine. I followed the footpath, and there was Annie, sitting under the maple tree. She was wearing a raincoat, so
I couldn't see her dress, and she had a scarf around her
head that also covered much of her face.

"This is a nice place," I said.

After a token smile she said, "Please sit down. I'm a
little nervous, and I want to talk to you." She was sitting
on a small stone bench. I sat next to her. She wouldn't
look at me directly when she started talking.

"On my summer vacation, when I was sixteen, I went
with my mother and father to Bavaria, because my father
loved climbing. He met a man at our hotel, and he and
this man would climb together. One day my father came
back very dizzy and had pains in his arm, which turned
out to be a heart attack. His friend carried him back to the
hotel and called a doctor, but my father died a few hours

later. This very helpful friend turned out to be Gustav
Gruner, a colonel in the German army."

The muscles in Annie's face were pulled tight. She still
didn't look at me.

"My mother was so upset that she wouldn't eat for several days. She just drank tea. I could see that Gustav was
attracted to my mother. He persuaded her to come—with
me—to his home in Karlsruhe, just to rest and recover.
She reluctantly agreed. When she started to feel better,
he took both of us to wonderful restaurants and we rode
bicycles together. Then he proposed marriage to my
mother. My father hadn't left us very much money and
Mother did like Gustav, so she said yes. After only a few
months she discovered that Gustav was faithless . . . like
most men, but not my father."

Tears were starting to drop from Annie's eyes, but her
voice remained strong. I didn't interrupt her to offer any
senseless words of wisdom.

"My mother was always very emotional. She attempted
suicide, with laudanum, but it failed. Gustav told her how
sorry he was, and he seemed genuinely apologetic. He suggested that Mother and I take a vacation in Italy, while he
was on manoeuvres. 'Allow me make it up to you,' he said.
'Please, let me send you to Rome, Siena, Florence . . . See
beautiful things and recover your health.' She reluctantly

agreed. When we returned from Italy, Mother found out that Gustav had taken a mistress."

This time Annie didn't speak for almost a minute. Then she cleared her throat and spoke again.

"When Gustav demanded sex from my mother, she took out a knife from under her pillow and tried to kill him. A few weeks later Gustav was promoted to general. The day that he was promoted, Mother took a very large dose of laudanum and this time she died, leaving me alone with Gen. Gustav Gruner. I was just eighteen and a virgin."

Her fists were clenched into tight balls as she continued.

"After the first time he raped me, I decided that trying to shoot him or take a knife to bed with me would probably fail. All my friends told me that war with France was inevitable, and that I had better stay put."

Annie turned and looked directly at me. She was extremely excited and had a strange smile on her face, but I didn't know if it was from anger or pleasure. It was almost as if she were telling me one of her favourite bedtime stories.

"So I began telling his own officers that General Gruner was a rapist," she said. "I told them to please be very discreet with what I was telling them, and *if* they were, I would reward them with my body. Each officer told me how discreet he had been, but I knew that rumours went around very quickly in the army, AND I WANTED THAT. I WAS COUNTING ON THAT. In a short while Gustav Gruner started to hear those rumours. He didn't come to my bedroom any more."

Annie took hold of my arm, and with a crooked smile she said, "I act like a whore, Monsieur Harry, because I am a whore. But I don't take money—I take revenge." She let go of my arm.

"Why do I tell you all this? I'm not sure, except that there was always something in the way you looked at me—even when I was angry with you—that I don't see in men. But if you don't want to see me again—that's all right."

As tears flowed from her eyes, she turned away. I put one arm around her, and she buried her head in my shoulder. I tried to imagine what these last years must have been like for her, but I couldn't.

While she cried, I looked up at the sky. Rain clouds were moving toward us. Because she was wearing a raincoat and a scarf, I assumed that Annie must have known it was going to rain. I looked down at a stone slab near my feet that had some writing carved into it.

*"How delightfully the fish are enjoying
themselves in the water," exclaimed
Chuangtse.*

*"You are not a fish," said his friend. "How
can you know they are enjoying themselves?"*

*"You are not me," replied Chuangtse. "How
can you know that I do not know that the
fish are enjoying themselves?"*

—*Chuangtse*

"Please go, Harry," Annie said, as she straightened up.
"I'd like to sit here for a while. You've been very kind."

I squeezed her hand lightly and left.

THIRTEEN

⌒

AFTER I RETURNED TO MY ROOM I POURED A SMALL
glass of sherry from a crystal decanter that was refilled each
day. I went to the window and watched the deer grazing
on the lawn under an apple tree, which was a safe-enough
distance from any humans. The fawns were eating apples
that weren't ripe yet, but which the mother deer managed
to reach with her long neck and pull down.

I went downstairs. When I found Viktor alone, I asked
him if he could possibly "loan" me some money. I made

up a cock 'n' bull story that, before I could get any of my secret funds from my secret bank, which was under my secret name, it would take weeks, and I wanted to buy some socks and undershorts and assorted things.

"Don't be ridiculous," he said, "of course you need money. I would be honoured." Five minutes later he handed me an envelope that was filled with German marks. It looked like it was much more than sufficient, but I was afraid to ask him how much one mark was worth. Then I called Annie.

When I heard her voice, I said, "I've just won a horse race and was handed a pile of money. Would you care to have dinner with me tonight?"

"What was the horse's name?" she asked.

"Asshole," I answered.

She had obviously never heard that word. "What does 'ash hole' mean?"

"Well, it means a kind of nice but stupid horse," I said.

"I see," she said. "And where would you like to have dinner?"

"Do you know a quiet restaurant that serves duck? I haven't eaten roast duck for almost two years now."

"Le Petit Bedon," she answered.

"Pardon?" I had no idea what she had just said.

"In French it means 'The Little stomach,'-" Annie explained. "You would probably say, 'The Little Tummy.' It's quite a small restaurant and very good."

"What time shall I pick you up?" I asked.

"Eight!"

"Good evening, Joseph," I said. He had now been assigned exclusively to me.

"Good evening, sir," he said with a little smile, happy, I think, that I continued to call him by his first name.

The bell outside of Annie's door sounded like a music box. Annie opened the door, not the maid. She was wearing a lavender dress, with little swirls of rose and blue, and . . . she wasn't wearing any make-up. When I saw her unpainted face, I was so moved that I was afraid I'd say the wrong thing. I certainly didn't want to embarrass her. It wasn't that Annie was suddenly beautiful; she was just nice looking, with a little nose, a tiny mouth, and very thin lips. With the thick make-up off of her face I could see that she had the fresh skin of a young girl, and, without all the mascara on her lashes, her greenish brown eyes looked terribly vulnerable. In that sense I did think she was beautiful.

I smiled and said, "I'm very happy to see you."

She nodded politely, but she seemed self-conscious. I had the feeling that she, also, didn't want to talk about the make-up. We stepped outside and into "my" auto. Annie gave Joseph the address and after about ten or twelve minutes we stopped in front of what looked like an ancient house.

"This is the oldest part of town," she said. "It dates back to the sixteenth century. I hope you like my little restaurant . . . and they do have duck tonight."

Joseph helped Annie out of the auto and we walked into "The Little Tummy." I told Annie I'd call it that because I felt awkward when I tried to say the French name. Not that I couldn't, I told her—I just didn't want to sound like a phony.

The owner came by to greet us and Annie introduced me. The owner was a round man, French, about sixty. Annie called him "Jamy." He had a nice smile, but I thought he looked a little sad. He and Annie talked in French for a minute and then Jamy said, in German (for my sake), that he would like to offer us some wine. I was afraid I was going to be put to another wine test, but then Jamy said, very proudly, "French wine! I still have some left in my cellar, but I can't get any more until this____war is over." (I knew what he said, even though he said it in French.)

The white wine he brought us was delicious. I thought Jamy said that the name of the wine was "Sincere" and when Annie heard me repeat it she let out a big laugh. When I asked if I had said it wrong, she said, "No, no—'Sincere' is perfect. You speak good French."

We both had duck with red cabbage, sautéed apples and little roast potatoes. I think it was the best meal I had ever eaten. After I looked at the bill, Annie helped me figure out how many marks I should leave.

As we were on our way out, I shook hands with Jamy and thanked him for the Sincere. Annie smiled when I said it, then she and the owner kissed each other on each cheek. He held her hands and looked into her eyes for several seconds and said something in French—I don't know whether it was about her not wearing make-up or if it was about me—whatever it was, he seemed to be happy for her.

We hardly spoke on the ride back to her apartment. I knew what I was thinking: I was afraid of not doing what I felt like doing . . . and afraid of doing it.

To break the silence I asked Annie which part of France she was from, as if I would know the difference whatever she answered. She said she was born in a tiny village that I wouldn't have heard of. It only had a thousand people, but it had a grade school and a church and a *tabac* shop for cigarettes, and a small brasserie, where you could sit and have a sandwich, an omelette, coffee, beer, whiskey, and orange drinks. It was mostly farmland around her home, she said. Her family moved to Paris when her father got a job with a company that made paper products.

When we arrived at Annie's apartment, she didn't make a move to get out of the auto—she just sat quietly, without looking at me.

"May I come up?" I asked.

She looked at me. For the first time since I met her, she seemed fragile. "Do you really want to?" she asked.

"Yes, I do."

She took out a key and opened the door to her apartment; again, no maid to greet us. I followed her into her bedroom. Annie took off her cloak. She didn't disappear into her bathroom this time—she just sat on the edge of her bed. I didn't want to make love with her—not this night—I just wanted to kiss her, which was something I understood more than lovemaking. I was afraid that if I made love, I would make a botch of it or else reach my climax too soon.

"Would you like something to drink?" she asked.

"No, thank you."

"What would you like, Harry?" she asked.

"I'd like to kiss you," I answered.

She got up and stood next to me. I touched her lips with my fingertips, as softly as I could. It was nice to actually see her lips. So much thinner than I thought they would be. I kissed her lips, very gently, but her muscles tightened and there seemed to be a struggle going on inside of her. Then I felt her nipples harden and she suddenly clung to me with so much force that it almost knocked the wind out of me. When I felt her open mouth on mine and her tongue touch my lips I became so overtaken with emotion that all of the meaningless thoughts that had been running through my head disappeared as suddenly as a lightning bolt. We helped each other off with our clothes quickly and clumsily. If we could have watched this scene in a silent movie, I'm sure we would have burst out laughing.

We made love intensely, without any thinking. Afterward I believe I was unconscious. I don't know for how long. When I returned to life I saw Annie lying next to me, very still, with her eyes closed. I leaned over and kissed her gently. Without opening her eyes, she pulled my head onto her chest.

When I got up to leave, Annie put on her robe and slippers and then helped me get dressed. She went outside with me and we kissed once more. The headlights from Joseph's Mercedes flashed on/off once, to let me know he was there. At her door, she kissed me one more time, and I left.

When I returned to my room, I tried to sleep, but I was too excited to let go of the night. I lay in bed reliving everything: her face without make-up, the smell of her body without the perfume, her small breasts, the sensation I felt when her tongue touched mine—which had never happened to me before—and what passion really was. When I finally fell asleep I dreamed that Elsie was crying and Wally and Murdock were still in the trench, but they were sitting up, eating duck. Even I could interpret that one.

FOURTEEN

⌒

I CALLED ANNIE THE NEXT MORNING AND ASKED IF SHE
had another restaurant I could take her to that would be
as good as last night's. She laughed and said, "I know one
such place. It's very quiet, very intimate."

"Good—where is it?" I asked.

"My place," she said. "But I'm sure you must be a very
difficult person to cook for."

"Not at all," I said. "Spaghetti, olive oil, and then throw
in anything else you want."

My heart filled with joy, I hung up and was about to eat my breakfast when I heard someone knocking on my door. It was Colonel Steinig's lieutenant, who asked if I could please join the colonel as soon as possible. I gobbled down my breakfast, put on one of my uniforms, and hurried downstairs. Steinig was waiting for me in the hallway.

"Harry," he said, without his usual smile, "could I impose upon you to join me on a duty which I hate, but which I'm obligated to perform?" I told him that if I could be of any real help, I would be happy to join him.

We drove for over an hour, but Steinig hardly said a word. I took a glance at the papers he was studying so seriously, but all I could make out was a list of names, with brief descriptions under each name. I didn't ask any questions.

His Mercedes came to a halt near what looked to be one of the German trenches. When we got out I saw six young German soldiers, tied to wooden posts that had been pounded into the ground. It looked like they were going to be crucified.

Steinig spoke for a few minutes to the commanding officer and then walked back to me.

"This is our field punishment," he said. "The Americans and the British use it, too, as a way of treating cowardice. Our commanding officers are finding it more and more difficult to keep spirits up and to stop desertions, so we do this in public to drive in the message to other soldiers."

"Are you going to flog them?" I asked.

"No, they're going to be shot," he said, "by men they've known and worked with. I don't like it, but it's absolutely necessary or there would be chaos. You certainly must understand this."

My mind raced. *I should be up there with them, I'm a coward, too . . . and I deserted . . . but instead of being shot, I'm making love and eating duck.*

I walked closer to the row of crosses, close enough to see the tears from several of the young soldiers. A sergeant came up to each of them and tied a white cloth around their heads, covering their eyes. One of the soldiers couldn't help crying "Papa" out loud. "Too late for Papa," the Sergeant answered as he put the white cloth around the boy's head.

Steinig nodded his head to the commanding officer, who shouted orders to a small group of soldiers who were standing at ease with their rifles. They quickly came to attention. My knees went limp. The soldiers raised their rifles and, upon hearing the command, shot their comrades.

As we walked back to his Mercedes, Steinig said, "It's an awful thing, but it brings across the message very clearly."

On the car ride home, Steinig was deep in thought. He didn't look at me or talk to me—which was very unlike him; he just stared out of his window. I finally asked, "Why did you want me to come with you, Viktor?"

He didn't say anything for the longest time, as if he were trying to decide whether he should answer my question. The thought raced through my mind that he knew the truth about me—that I was pretending to be Harry Stroller, and that this was his way of saying that he knew but wasn't sure what to do about it—how it might damage Germany, and his own reputation, to have been taken in by a simpleton from America. He finally spoke:

"It may sound strange to you . . . but I don't really have friends, Harry—not what I would call *real* friends. You turned out to be very different from the famous Harry Stroller I had imagined—much more human than all of my aristocrats and generals. I wanted you to come with me because I wanted a friend near me when I had to execute still another group of young cowards. Does that answer your question?"

I nodded yes and rode back to Karlsruhe deep in thought.

When Annie opened the door, she knew immediately that something was wrong. She hugged me and said, "Such worries I see in your face. Come in, dear." She led me into her apartment. I sat at her small kitchen table, where a bottle of wine had already been opened. She poured a glass for me. I took a sip and said, "That's just what I needed."

"Do you know what you're drinking?"

I took another sip, this time concentrating, as if I were one of those real wine experts. Then my face lit up. "Sincere!"

"Yes. You are so smart. It's one of Jamy's last bottles, but he insisted."

After I took a few more sips, Annie said, "What's the matter? Are you not allowed to tell me?" She asked so sweetly that it almost brought tears to my eyes, I suppose because it reminded me of my mother, hugging and kissing me when I came home crying if the boys in the neighbourhood had beaten me up.

I told Annie what I had seen that day. She stared at the kitchen table for the longest time, holding back her own tears. Then she got up with a big smile and told me to wait in the kitchen until she called for me. I had images of her coming out naked and taking me to bed, but I was wrong. I heard the bathtub running and after three or four minutes she called out, "Come in here, please!"

When I walked into her bathroom there were ten or twelve candles, all lit, resting on the wide edge of her large bathtub, which was filled with hot water. She helped me off with my uniform and into the tub. She hummed a pretty melody as she scrubbed my body with an enormous sponge that was filled with nice-smelling soap.

When my bath was over she wrapped a large towel around me and led me into the bedroom. "Lie down while I cook our dinner," she said. She turned the lamp down and I fell into a deep sleep. When I woke up it was only because I heard Annie hollering from the kitchen, "Your dinner is ready, Signore."

I walked into the kitchen. The little table was set with simple country pottery, blue-and-white cloth napkins, two wine glasses, and two water glasses. A bottle of red wine was open.

"Don't worry," she said, "the red wine is French. Not expensive, but honest. Do you like country wines?"

I had no idea what "country wines" were. I knew wine didn't grow in the city, so I assumed it must come from the country, but I didn't want to sound dumb, so I said, "Oh yes, they're wonderful."

Annie set a large bowl of spaghetti on the table. It was filled with bits of chicken, a little sausage, cauliflower, white beans, peas, and golden brown sautéed garlic. She also put a beautiful wooden bowl on the table that was stuffed with all kinds of lettuce. She said, "The salad is for later, with cheese—that way you'll eat like a Frenchman." When I told her that I had never seen a wooden bowl like the one the salad was in, she said it was made from an olive tree.

I ate like a man who had just been rescued from a desert island. I had three helpings of spaghetti. When I interrupted my gobbling and looked up, I could see that Annie was enjoying watching me eat.

"You like my cooking?"

"I like *you*—the cooking is okay. I'm just not very hungry today."

I returned her smile. Then I said, "This country wine is about the best I've ever had."

Annie said, "May I ask you a very serious question?"

"Of course."

"Do you really like me so much more without my whore's make-up?"

Careful . . . Careful . . . don't hurt her. . . . "You're the same woman, Annie . . . but now I can see how beautiful you are."

"I'm not beautiful. I know that. But it fills my heart that you think I am."

"Well, I don't know what you think 'beautiful' means—I suppose everyone has a different idea. I think it's something that's half on the outside and half on the inside. Without all that make-up on your face—I can see the inside a little better. That doesn't hurt your feelings, does it?"

"No, dear, it doesn't," and then she got up and sat on my lap. "Am I too heavy for you?"

"Never."

"Is your name really Harry?"

Her question caught me so much by surprise that I felt as if the wind had been knocked out of me. I wasn't sure what to answer. I wanted to tell her everything, but what danger would I be putting both of us in if I told her the truth? . . . I'm not Harry Stroller . . . I'm not a spy . . . I'm not German . . . I'm an American soldier . . . just a coward who ran away . . . and can be clever once in a while.

Annie must have seen my quandary because she said, "It's all right, dear—you don't have to answer. I'm sorry."

"No, I want to tell you all kinds of things, Annie, but what made you ask that question?"

"Well . . . you just don't look like a 'Harry.'-"

I was dumbstruck. I wanted to laugh, but I held it in.

"And that's the only reason you asked?"

"Yes. Did that upset you, sweetheart?"

"No, not at all. To tell you the truth, I've had lots of names in the last few months. You can call me Harry, or Franz, or Paul . . . but I do like 'sweetheart' the best."

"All right, sweetheart. Well, I didn't know if you wanted to see me tomorrow, but—"

"Yes, I do."

She smiled and gave me a hug. "I'm only asking because there's going to be a small birthday party for one of Jamy's daughters tomorrow night at the restaurant, and I promised weeks ago that I'd come. Today I was going to ask you to come with me, but then I thought your superiors might not like it if they knew you attended a party surrounded only by French people. Was I wrong?"

"No, you were right. Unfortunately. Well, I'll just have to live through one night without you."

After dinner we went back to her bed. I tried to make love, but couldn't. I kept thinking about those young soldiers who were shot. Annie said, "That's all right, dear—just rest."

I fell asleep while I was hugging her.

Sometime after midnight Joseph drove me back to Colonel Steinig's castle. I went to sleep again, somewhat at peace.

FIFTEEN

WHEN I SAW JOSEPH THE NEXT MORNING, I ASKED IF HE was going to be busy that night.

"Sir," he said, "I have no obligation except to serve you."

"Well, how would you like to have dinner with me tonight?"

"Oh sir, I don't think . . ."

"Good! Don't think! That's best. I want you to take me to your favourite restaurant. I pay, but you choose the restaurant. Your favourite!"

"Oh sir, how can—"

"That's an order. I'm a colonel; you're a corporal."

"Yes sir," he said with a smile.

"And don't wear a uniform," I said.

That night Joseph picked me up at seven thirty and drove us to a small restaurant called The Heidelberg, which was near Karlsruhe's theatre district. I liked the smell of the place as soon as we walked in: sauerkraut, sausages, and meats that were being slow roasted. It reminded me of one of the German restaurants in Milwaukee—the only thing missing was a piano, a violin, and a cello, playing Schubert.

I was wearing a light blue summer suit that "my tailor" fixed up for me, and Joseph looked very handsome in a tan summer suit. Without his corporal's hat on, I could see his beautiful silver hair and his tired blue eyes.

There were two adjoining rooms in the restaurant, one larger and one that was quite private, with only four tables. I'm sure Joseph must have called ahead and requested this more private room. I spoke only German with Joseph. When the waiter came over, I asked Joseph what he was going to drink.

"Beer, sir."

"Order me the same, whatever you're having. And order dinner for me, too—whatever your favourite dishes are."

Joseph told the waiter that he wanted two steins of Pils and *kalbsaxe* for two. When the waiter left, I turned to Joseph and spoke softly:

"Joseph, please don't call me 'sir' while we're here."

"But I have to, sir."

"I'll make a bargain with you: How about if I call you 'Joe' and you call me 'Harry?'-"

"I couldn't do that, sir."

"All right, I'll call you Joe and you call me Herr Harry."

Joseph laughed and said, "I just cannot do that, sir."

"All right—this is my final offer: I'll call you Joseph and you call me Herr Stroller—just for tonight. Is that a deal?"

He smiled and said, "Yes, Herr Stroller."

A huge stein of beer was placed in front of me. The beer was wonderful—very much like a lager—but I had never tasted a beer this good in Milwaukee, even if that is where beer comes from. The *kalbsaxe,* which is a veal shank, was big enough for three or four hungry men. It was good enough to win a prize at the Wisconsin State Fair.

We didn't talk about the war or politics when anyone was near, and then only in hushed tones, but I got the strong impression that Joseph was against the war and thought it was all because of ignorant politicians, French and German.

"Do you have a family, Joseph?"

"I sent them as far away from the front as I could. My cousin has a small farm outside of Magdeburg. I want them to be safe."

"May I ask how old you are?"

"I'm sixty-three, Herr Stroller. I don't know where all the years have gone . . . they seem to have flown away, like pigeons."

We had some coffee and strudel for dessert.

On the ride back to the castle, Joseph talked about his wife and children, and love, and then—whether it was because he was thinking of his wife, or thinking of Annie and me, or if it was because of all the beer he had drunk—he began to sing.

> *"Ich hab' mein Herz in Heidelberg verloren,*
> *In einer lauen Sommernacht,*
> *Ich war verliebt bis uber beide Ohren . . ."*

I burst out laughing. "What on earth did you just

sing?"

"I lost my heart in Heidelberg, on a warm summer night—it's a drinking song."

"No, I mean—that last line—I fell in love *with my ears?*"

Joseph laughed. "No, no—I fell in love *over my ears.*"

I sat back and said, *"I fell in love 'over my ears,'"* quietly to myself.

When we arrived at Viktor's castle, Joseph opened the car door for me.

"Good night, Joseph," I said, "and thank you."

"Good night, sir," he answered.

After I went to bed I couldn't fall asleep. I wouldn't say it out loud, even to myself, but I was too happy to sleep. Of course, because I was happy, Wally and Murdock popped into my head. I allowed myself the luxury of shutting them out, at least for a little while, because I was sure they'd be glad for me. So go to sleep, Peachy. Go to sleep.

One night without her and I feel lost. That's not logical. But if I were logical, would I be here? Think of something nice. Think of Annie. I'd like to be with her someplace where people would pass us by and I would nod hello and pretend that we were just ordinary people, holding hands as we walked.

SIXTEEN

⌒

I WOKE UP EARLY. WHEN I FINISHED MY BREAKFAST OF farmer's cheese, dark bread, and coffee, I called Annie and asked if she were free and would she like to take a walk with me in some pretty place, and did she know how much I missed her after not having seen her for such a long time. She said she knew of a nice place to walk, and "Thank you, sweetheart." I knew she said "sweetheart" so often because I had told her that of all my names, "sweetheart" was my favourite.

Joseph dropped us off at the entrance to the Stadtgarten. It was a nice park, just on the edge of town. A branch of the river Lauter ran alongside it, and several couples were paddling their rented rowboats up and down this little tributary. Annie looked so pretty in what I imagined was one of her French dresses from years ago . . . lavender and flowered with blue and pink. She also wore a little straw hat that had a small, rose-coloured bow in the front. It was a sunny day, warm but not hot, and ideal for hand holding.

In the distance I saw a man and a woman coming toward us. I saw that the man was in uniform and that he and his lady were in their mid-thirties, but what I couldn't see, until they were almost next to us, was that the soldier was a corporal and only had half of his right arm. As we passed each other the soldier raised his elbow smartly, as if he had forgotten that there wasn't a hand attached, and he saluted me. I saluted back and nodded a hello to him. I instinctively stopped holding Annie's hand.

Annie squeezed my arm. "I'm sorry—this isn't what I expected when I suggested we walk in the Stadtgarten."

"The crazy part is that he seemed so happy to salute

me," I said. "He should want to spit at me instead."

"Please forgive me," she said. "I thought this would be romantic."

A young soldier, no more than fifteen or sixteen years old, was walking toward us with his girlfriend. When he saw me he grabbed his girlfriend's hand and ran toward us so fast that his cap fell off. He made a half stop to pick up his cap and arrived in front of us with a huge smile. He quickly snapped to attention and gave me a smart salute. He was so proud to be *one of us*. When I returned his salute, he beamed. Without realizing how stupid it was, I said, "Be a good boy," and they both ran off like little lambs, stumbling over each other.

A woman was pushing a four-wheel cart toward us, but there wasn't a baby in this cart—it was a soldier, in his late twenties, who had lost both his legs. His back was propped up with pillows. The woman looked at me with such a poisonous smile that I thought for sure she was going to spit on me. The soldier, however, gave me a big smile and saluted smartly.

"Good day, Colonel," he said. I would guess that he was proud that a colonel had stopped to say hello to him. I returned his salute and just as I was about to say something I thought would be cheerful, the woman—his wife I assumed—said, "It's a wonderful day for walking, isn't it Colonel?" Before I could answer she quickly pushed the cart past me. I didn't blame her. If I were free to speak, I would have told her that I felt the same way.

When Annie saw how upset I was, she took my arm and pulled me away. "Come, dear, I want to show you something."

She led me back toward the entrance to the park, and then along a dirt path that led to a large tent. An elderly ticket taker was sitting on a stool at the entrance to the tent.

"How much do I give him?" I asked.

"Twenty *pfennig* is fine for the two of us."

"How much is that worth?"

"You can buy two eggs with it, or a loaf of bread," she said. "Each year it's worth less and less."

"Does he get to keep the money?"

"Half of it. The other half goes to the actors."

My heart jumped a beat. "What actors?"

"They're very small actors, dear. Don't be impatient— you'll see."

I reached into my pocket and gave the old man a one-half mark coin and told him not to give me any change. His eyes lit up.

"Dank, mein Herr. Schoenen dank."

As we started to push our way through the entrance

flaps, I asked Annie how much half a mark was worth.

"A dozen eggs and a loaf of bread. It was very nice of you, sweetheart."

When we were inside the tent I saw that a puppet show was in progress. I let out a small squeal, like a child seeing a Christmas toy. Annie started to giggle. "Didn't I tell you the actors were small?"

The tent was filled with benches—the ones nearest to the stage were packed with children sitting with their mouths open in anticipation. Annie and I sat on a bench near the rear of the tent, along with the other adults. When the girl puppet, high in a little tower, started lowering her long, blonde hair down to the waiting prince, I realised that we were watching the fairy tale, "Rapunzel."

"Do you know 'Rapunzel'?" I whispered.

"I don't remember anything except how frightened I was when my mother read it to me," Annie whispered.

I knew the basic plot, but this German version we were watching was bizarre, because every time the handsome young prince tried to climb up Rapunzel's hair to rescue her, Rapunzel bopped him on the head, and each time she bopped him, the children screamed with laughter. After a while, Annie and I couldn't help laughing along with them. Pretty clever, I thought.

"Who are these actors?" I whispered.

"Both of them are women," Annie whispered, "and they're both the daughters of the old man you gave half a mark to. He also made the puppets and writes the stories."

When this much-abbreviated version of "Rapunzel" was over, a curtain came down and the children applauded. On our way out I shook hands with the old man and congratulated him.

It was only 11:00 a.m. Annie suggested that we go back to her apartment and have a sandwich. When we were in her living room, Annie said, with a tiny smile, "Now tell me—what do you really feel like? I have liver sausage, some cold chicken, some spaghetti that you didn't finish—"

"I'll give you three guesses what I really want," I answered.

She beamed. "Now let me see . . . the chicken?"

"No. . . ."

"The spaghetti?"

"No. . . ."

"Don't tell me it's the liver sausage?" she asked.

"No!"

"Well, I give up," she said. "What in the world could it be?"

"A haircut!" I answered.

She laughed so loud that I almost choked. I had never heard her truly laugh since I met her.

"Are you serious?" she asked.

"Very serious. It was brought to my attention yesterday that I don't exactly look like a colonel when I have this hair falling over my collar in the back."

"Come with me, please," she said.

She led me into the kitchen. "Take off your shirt, please." She went into the bathroom and came out with a big towel, which she spread onto the kitchen floor. She placed a chair on top of the towel.

"Sit down, please."

When I sat down, she gave me a quick kiss and began snipping away at my hair. "I thought you were going to ask for something else," she said.

"I thought of that too—but I think this is more important, don't you?"

"Well, I certainly wouldn't want you to get into trouble with your generals. How would it look if Harry Stroller, the famous spy, had hair that was one centimetre too long in the back? They might make you a private again."

Careful, Peachy . . . don't show it on your face. "That would be embarrassing," I said. "They might also take away my visiting privileges."

Annie sat on my lap. "All done!"

"Already?"

"One centimetre doesn't take very long to cut."

"All right," I said, "now what can I do for you?"

She smiled, gave me a loving kiss, and then said, "A haircut!"

"Are you joking?"

"No, I need a haircut, too—but just a little one. Eva, the lady who cuts my hair, has gone to visit her father for two weeks. So . . . can you cut my hair, Monsieur?"

"Yes! I happen to be a very good hair cutter. You can ask my dog. Please sit down."

She sat down.

"Do you want music?" I asked.

"Oh yes. Please," she said.

I began cutting her hair, very carefully, as I sang, "If you were the only girl in the world, and I were—"

There was a knock on the door. Annie got up while I put my shirt on. It was Joseph.

"I'm so sorry to disturb you, sir, mademoiselle—"

"That's all right, Joseph. Is something wrong?" I asked.

"Colonel Steinig sent a messenger to me. He asks if you would please come to see him as soon as possible. It's something urgent. I'm so sorry for interrupting you, sir."

"That's quite all right, Joseph. Do you have any idea

what the urgency is about?" I asked, as I finished tucking in my shirt and putting on my jacket as Annie helped with my tie.

"I have no idea, sir. The messenger only asked that I give you the message."

"I'll be down in a minute."

"Yes sir. Thank you. Good day, mademoiselle." Joseph left.

I turned to Annie. "I'll see you soon."

"I'll be here."

SEVENTEEN

⌒

WHEN I WALKED INTO STEINIG'S STUDY HE ROSE QUICKLY, wished me a "Good morning," and said that it was time to put me to work.

"What is it you want me to do?" I asked—"More Shakespeare?"

"It's a surprise, Harry. You'll see," he answered, with a quizzical smile.

A little panic rushed by. "Did someone ask for me?"

"They all ask for you, Harry. You're famous now. That's

because you have a good manager."

"Maybe I don't pay you enough," I said, trying to disguise my nervousness.

"Up until now I've indulged you, Harry. I've also been boasting about you to every officer in my command. But now I want to see the real Harry Stroller in action. No more showing off at dinner parties—I want to see the 'Master' at work."

"I hope I don't disappoint you," I said.

"So do I," Steinig said, "because I want you to meet a special guest of ours."

"Someone big?" I asked.

"Not so big . . . but he's an American."

We drove for about twenty minutes and arrived in Birkenfeld, a small and not very attractive town. We walked past the town square and into a prison that must have been a hundred years old. We stopped at the reception booth, where the sergeant on duty saluted us both, and then we walked down a flight of stairs into what seemed like a cellar.

It was fairly dark inside, cold and damp, and smelled terribly. It took awhile for my eyes to adjust. Then I saw a short, comical-looking man in a major's uniform, standing next to what appeared to be a wounded prisoner who was slumped over in a chair. A well-built guard stood behind him, holding a rifle. When the prisoner looked up, I saw that it was Captain Harrington.

"Peachy," he said in a hoarse voice, unaware, I think, that he had spoken. He seemed as startled to see me as I was to see him. He looked so thin and his hands and face seemed slightly blue.

Feeling panic in my throat, I shouted, in English:

"NOT A WORD! DON'T OPEN YOUR MOUTH— BECAUSE I DON'T WANT TO HEAR IT!"

He looked confused, but I had to keep him from saying anything else, for both our sakes.

"*THEY* WANT YOU TO SPEAK—I DON'T! SO IF YOU WANT TO LIVE—KEEP YOUR GODDAMN MOUTH SHUT!"

I turned to the major and spoke in German.

"Was he alone?"

"Yes sir."

"What has he told you?"

"Nothing, sir—he hasn't spoken a word—not even his name. He must have been shot in the leg when the Americans attacked two weeks ago. Two of our soldiers found him lying unconscious in the middle of all the dead and wounded bodies between our trenches and theirs.

When they saw that he was a kapitan they dragged him across the field to our trenches. Either his dog tags broke off as they dragged him or he threw them away, but they thought that if he really was a kapitan they should bring him in."

"That was smart. Has he had medical attention?" I asked.

"One of our doctors treated his leg wound, but that's all, sir," the major answered.

"Why do you have him in this rotten cellar?" I asked.

"For interrogation only, sir—otherwise we keep him in a cell upstairs, in the main part of the prison. It has guards on duty at all times."

"Good."

"There has been a general attack in the region for the past three weeks, sir," the major said. "Our Intelligence believes this is only a diversion—just to draw our reserves away from the area of their main attack—but we don't know where or when that will be. That is what we were hoping this prisoner would tell us."

I walked up to Captain Harrington. He looked weak, but I could see that the spirit was still in his eyes and so was the little black hair coming out of the wart on his nose. I had no idea what to do. I tried to keep my pity from showing, so I started to babble away, in English, stalling for time until I could think of something.

"You've had your hair cut recently, Captain," I said, remembering very well when we all had our last haircut because the young barber nicked a piece of my ear and made it bleed.

"Your hair is still uneven on the right side of your head—probably because you had it cut by some fool private who wants to be a barber."

Steinig had a strange look on his face, trying to figure out what the hell I was doing. I was trying to figure that out, too.

"I would guess that your hair has only been cut once since you've arrived in France," I said, "probably the Sunday before last, since I understand that all of you like to get your haircuts every other Sunday, after supper. You have more rituals in your army than we do."

I glanced at Steinig, who looked terribly disappointed.

"So," I said, having found my inspiration, "since your regiment couldn't have been at the front for more than three weeks . . . that means . . . that you must have sailed from New York at 6:30 a.m. on the 14th of May . . . and landed at Saint-Nazaire at noon on June 1st."

I thought Major Heintz's jaw was going to fall off of his face. Steinig looked on with wonder.

"To my knowledge, the only American Division that

landed in France in the last three weeks is the 2nd, com-manded by Maj. Gen. O. for "OK" Barker . . . and the only regiment in the Second Division—close enough to where you were captured—is the Ninth Regiment . . . and the Ninth Regiment has made up a song—*which I have heard*—about one of it's company commanders who has a small black hair coming out of a wart on his nose. So—I advise you to keep on your toes, CAPT. JOHN 'HAIR NOSE' HARRINGTON FROM RHINELANDER, WISCONSIN!"

Now Steinig was stunned. The major covered his mouth with both hands.

As I looked at Captain Harrington I tried to develop a nervous wink in my left eye.

"Now listen to me carefully, Captain Harrington, *if* you want to live. For three weeks there has been a general attack in this region, but this is only a diversion, am I right?"

Captain Harrington rose to the occasion. "Yes," he said, with a very serious face.

"The main attack will be in quite a different place—is that not right, Captain?"

"Yes."

"Where?"

The major and Steinig leaned forward slightly.

"Switzerland," Harrington answered.

I was so shocked at his answer that I blurted out, "SWITZERLAND??"

"Yes," he said.

The major said, "Sir, General Hoffman always insisted that we could outflank the French line by driving through Switzerland, but no one took him seriously."

Recovering from my near disaster, I said, "Hoffman is a good man. You had all better start listening to him." Then I turned back to Captain Harrington.

"Captain, this is only the beginning. I'll be seeing you again very soon."

"Major!" I called out as I walked over to him. He quickly came to attention.

"Sir!" he said.

"What's your name?" I asked.

"Heintz, sir."

Then I spoke in a soft voice, almost a whisper, as if I didn't want the prisoner to hear us. "What have you been feeding this man?"

"Mostly hard biscuits and water," Heintz whispered. "We thought that if he were hungry enough, and tired, he might start talking. It usually works, sir."

"Wrong!" I whispered, as if I were talking to a nincompoop. "That's just what he wants. He's trying to be a hero, don't you see? The only way to reach a man like this is to soften him up, put him off his guard."

"Yes sir," he said, with a questioning look.

"Give him some hot soup tonight."

"Yes sir."

"And some duck."

"Duck?" Heintz whispered, unbelievingly.

"Yes, duck—of course," I whispered, "with red cabbage and some of those tiny roast potatoes. And give him very cold Champagne, even if he doesn't want it, but you have to insist. Even force it on him. Is that clear?"

"Yes sir."

I put my arm around Heintz's shoulder and whispered, as if to a young student, "You understand what I'm trying to do, don't you, Heintz?"

"Oh yes, sir," Heintz said with a smile.

"If I should want to interrogate him again, which cell is he in?" I whispered, even more softly.

"Cell number fourteen, sir," he whispered.

"What time do you go off duty, Heintz?"

"At nineteen hundred hours, sir, when they change guards. But of course, if you should need me—"

"No, no—nothing now—only when a good idea strikes me. Let's wait a few days—then we'll see what he has to say."

"Yes sir."

I returned to my normal voice:

"All right—I'm finished!"

I walked over to Steinig, who greeted me with a big smile and said, "Harry—if I hadn't seen it, I wouldn't have believed it."

"I know how you feel," I answered.

As we left the cellar, I took one more look at Captain Harrington. I thought I saw a hint of a smile on his face.

My legs were trembling when we walked into the sunlight. I was so tense when I saw Captain Harrington, and so afraid of making some horrible error, that all my muscles tightened into knots. I tried to hide my nervousness on the ride back, making small talk with Viktor Steinig, even ridiculing what a simpleton the prisoner was.

When we returned to his *schloss,* Steinig said he was going to have a working lunch with his staff and that I was welcome to join them, but he thought it would be a little boring after what he had just seen this morning.

"I'm sure you're right," I said, and thanked him.

I went up to my room and tried to think of some plan to save Captain Harrington, but the only ideas that came to me were bad ones and completely unrealistic. I couldn't overpower two or three guards. I couldn't overpower even one of them. I knew that the best time to do anything would be just after Heintz left, at 1900 hours—seven o'clock—but no ideas came. I decided to take a walk in the woods, hoping that without distractions, other than the birds and the deer, some inspiration might come.

On my way out of the *schloss* I saw Steinig's staff arriving—captains, majors, and colonels, along with their aides. The colonels were getting out of motorcycle sidecars, which were driven by their aides, mostly corporals, who were wearing long, beige riding jackets. The inspiration didn't hit until I saw some of them taking off their goggles. All the aides were standing together, waiting, as they gossiped and smoked cigarettes. One of them noticed me and started to throw his cigarette away.

"No, it's quite all right, Corporal," I said—"I was just admiring your motorcycle."

"Yes, sir. It's an *Alba*, sir," he said. "She's a beauty, isn't she?"

"She certainly is."

As I walked around his Alba, pretending to be an expert, I remembered my passion for motorcycles from my teenage days. I had wanted one so badly, but I couldn't afford to buy one. My best friend, Artie, used to let me ride his. He had to work every other Saturday, so on those days he let me take his cycle on long trips in the country.

"Do you need a key for ignition or just a pedal?" I asked.

"With the Alba we just have to pump the pedal a few times and off we go."

"Wonderful! Where do all of you park these beautiful machines when your work is done?" I asked.

"Just north of here, sir—about a kilometre—just behind the old church," he answered.

"Please, relax now—enjoy your smoke. I shouldn't be bothering you—this is your time off."

"Thank you, sir. Very kind of you," he said.

I rushed back to my room, put a pair of military trousers in my briefcase, took the pistol out of my underwear drawer and placed it in my briefcase. Then I walked outside again.

I passed Steinig's aide, who was standing on the steps, ushering in the last of the staff.

"Lieutenant," I said.

He saluted. "Sir!"

"Would you tell Colonel Steinig that I'm going for a walk this afternoon and that I'll be dining with Mademoiselle Breton this evening?"

"Of course, sir," he said.

I walked away, heading north toward the old church.

When I saw it, I couldn't understand why the corporal referred to it as the "old" church, since all the churches in Karlsruhe were ancient. This church was only a short walk from Annie's apartment. I remembered hearing the church bells only too well, as they rang loudly every fifteen minutes, sometimes at the most intimate moments.

I walked a little farther and saw a sign that read:

MOTORRAD PARKHAUS

I walked onto the grounds and saw three or four cycles parked there, but only two of them had sidecars. The other cycles must have been at the staff meeting, resting near the drivers who were waiting for their colonels to come out.

An overweight guard with mustard on his chin hurried out of a small cabin and saluted me. He had a napkin tucked into his uniform. I told him I was a newcomer to Karlsruhe and was just inspecting the grounds. "Please, don't disturb yourself," I said. "Enjoy your lunch."

"Thank you, Colonel," he said, saluted me once more and went back into his cabin to finish eating.

As I walked around the grounds I came across what looked like a locker room. When I walked in I saw that there were toilets, showers, bottles of shampoo, towels, colognes, and even mats on the floor so that the drivers wouldn't have to walk barefoot on the cement. Everything was spotlessly clean. Then I saw what I was looking for—a rack containing goggles, drivers' caps, gloves, and the long, beige riding jackets that all the drivers were wearing at Steinig's *schloss*. Everything seemed to be communal, because there were no names or numbers printed above them.

I quickly took a pair of goggles, tried on a few caps until I found one that fit me, took a beige riding jacket and a pair of gloves, and squeezed all of it into my briefcase, with my Lugar resting on top. I walked out, slowly.

When I was back in my room I took a pair of black socks from my drawer and, with my razor, cut out a crude eye patch that I hoped would look like the ones that so many German officers were wearing to cover an eye that they had lost in battle. I think they also thought that it was a sign of distinction, like a medal.

Early that evening Joseph drove me to Annie's apartment. I was wearing my dress uniform and carried my precious briefcase. I told Joseph to take his time and have a leisurely dinner; then come back and wait for me outside of Mademoiselle's apartment.

"I may be a very long time tonight, Joseph," I said with a little smile.

"I understand, Herr Stroller," he answered, with a slight twinkle in his eyes.

I told Joseph to enjoy his dinner and walked up the stairs to Annie's apartment.

She knew something was wrong the moment she opened the door. I must have looked like I was going to a parade, wearing my dress uniform and carrying a briefcase—not exactly how she was used to seeing me when I came to visit. She always seemed to know what was going on inside my brain, and my heart, when she looked at my eyes. She took my briefcase, and then my hand, and led me into the living room. When we stood facing each other, she kissed me gently. Feeling her lips again, I suddenly hugged her with so much force that I apologised, afraid that I might have hurt her.

"You'll never hurt me that way," she said. "Can you tell me what's wrong?"

"If I tell you that only the most urgent crisis could keep me from seeing you tonight, would you believe me?"

"Of course I would, dear. Can you come later?"

"I'm not sure how long I'll be."

"If you can, will you come back to see me? No matter how late it is? Even if I'm asleep? . . . Will you come
back?"

"Yes, I will."

EIGHTEEN

⌒

I NEEDED TO CHANGE COSTUMES SOMEWHERE SECLUDED.
I asked Annie if there was a place I could leave her apartment without being seen. She showed me the stairway she used at the back of her building which led to a parking area for tenants. I gave her a quick kiss good-bye and waited until she went back into her apartment.

On the stairway I took out the goggles, cap, and long riding jacket from my briefcase and put them on. The beige jacket covered my colonel's uniform. I put my col-

onel's hat into the briefcase. The church bells gonged: it
was 6:45 p.m.

I walked into the Motorrad Parkhaus and started ex-
amining cycles with sidecars. A new guard appeared out
of nowhere and started asking me questions.

"I'm supposed to pick up Colonel von Rieger, immediately, and I have no time for stupid questions," I barked.
"Tell me if you have an Alba available that's been filled
with petrol."

He looked at me with a puzzled face.

"Idiot—the colonel is waiting."

The guard rushed over to a cycle with sidecar and said
he had filled the tank two hours ago. It was an Alba. I
didn't bother thanking him—that might have made him
suspicious. I got on the seat, put my briefcase in the wire
basket behind me, pumped the pedal three times and the
motor started. I tried to look as professional as possible as
I drove off, but the first five or ten seconds were almost a
disaster. I jerked and stopped, and jerked and stopped. I
knew how to ride a motorcycle, but the sudden burst of
speed from this cycle nearly made me capsize. When I finally adjusted to the temperament of the Alba, I zoomed
out of the Parkhaus.

I remembered the route Steinig and I had taken to Birkenfeld and I stopped about a hundred yards short of the prison. It was 7:15 p.m. and not really dark yet, but dark enough. I took out my eye patch and colonel's hat from my briefcase, then took off my riding coat, goggles and corporal's cap and put them into the briefcase. I tied the eye patch over my right eye, put my colonel's hat on, and walked slowly to the entrance of the prison, carrying my briefcase.

When I arrived at the reception desk, the guard on duty was, as I expected, eating his dinner. He jumped up from his desk when he saw me and saluted.

"Get me Major Heintz," I said in German.

"I'm sorry, sir—he left half an hour ago."

"*Scheisse,*" I said. I almost said "shit" but caught myself in time.

"I can call him, sir, if you like," the guard said.

"No, never mind," I said. "Let him eat his dinner. And you as well. I'm Colonel von Rieger—give me the key to cell fourteen."

"Yes sir," he said. "Would you sign this book please, Colonel?"

Under the date, I signed:

Colonel von Rieger—19:30 hours

He pulled a key off of a hook and handed it to me. "It's on the second floor, sir."

"My driver is having a sandwich at the Konditorei," I said. "I told him to fetch me in twenty minutes. Direct him to cell fourteen as soon as he arrives."

"Yes sir," he said, still standing at attention.

"Eat your dinner," I said. "Everyone else is."

"Thank you, sir."

I went up to the second floor and walked down a dark aisle that was stifling because of the heat and mustiness. When I arrived at cell fourteen I saw a tall guard sitting on a chair a few cells farther down the aisle. When he saw me, he quickly rose.

"Sir, do you want me to—"

"I have the key. What's your name?"

"Krauss, sir."

"My driver will be here in approximately twenty minutes. If I need you, I'll call."

"Yes sir," he said.

I opened the cell door and saw Captain Harrington sitting on a small bench next to a cot. I suddenly turned to the guard and said, "Get me a bar of soap and a clean towel."

"Sir, the morning crew does all of those—"

"NOW! I want them NOW!" I shouted.

Right away, sir." And he hurried down the stairs.

I walked into the cell. Captain Harrington didn't recognise me, of course. When I took the patch off, he said, "Peachy!"

I signalled "Shh" with one finger and immediately started taking off my uniform jacket. I spoke in a whisper as I took the pair of military trousers out of my briefcase.

"Put this jacket on, sir, and these trousers."

He took off his torn and filthy trousers and put on the new ones. Then he put on my colonel's jacket.

"What in God's name are we doing?" he whispered.

"I can't explain anything now, sir, but please hurry."

As he was dressing, I took out the long, beige rider's jacket and the cap and put them on. I tied the black eye patch over Captain Harrington's right eye. I almost put it on his left eye, but caught myself in time. Then I put the colonel's hat on his head.

"Don't say anything, sir. If anyone speaks, just look perturbed or angry. I'll do the explaining. Clear?"

"Yes."

"And when we walk out of the cell, *you* have to lock the cell door with this key."

I handed him the key and then opened the cell door just as the guard was rushing back with a bar of soap and a clean towel.

"He doesn't need that now," I said, changing my voice a few notes higher. "Colonel von Reiger has learned what he came here for."

"But, but—"

"Give him a dirty look, sir," I whispered.

Captain Harrington was a good actor. He turned and stared at the guard.

"Yes sir," the guard said.

We walked down the stairs. I carried the *colonel's* brief-case for him.

"At reception, hand the key to the guard and say, *'Danke,'-"* I told Captain Harrington.

When we reached reception, the guard, who was just finishing his dinner, jumped up. Captain Harrington tossed the key onto the desk, next to the 'sign in' book, and said, *"Danke."*

The guard answered, "Guten Abend, Herr Oberst," and we walked out onto the street.

"Turn left here, sir, then walk in front of me, straight ahead for about a hundred yards. A motorcycle and side-car are there. You can take off the eye patch now."

"Yes, sir, Private Peachy," he said, with a slight smile.

When we reached the Alba, it was quite dark. It was also a cloudy night, which I was thankful for. I assisted

Captain Harrington into the sidecar and got onto the cycle, pumped the start pedal three times . . . and nothing happened. My heart sank. I pumped three more times and heard a little sputtering. On my third try the motor roared, and I took off quickly.

We couldn't talk on the way because the noise from the motor and the wind made it impossible. I was glad of that. When we passed a road sign that read SAARBRÜCKEN, I pulled over and came to a halt. There was a German guardhouse nearby, so I left the motor idling. I got off and unscrewed the facing of the cycle's headlight so that it would look like I was fixing something, just in case a guard came by. Lights from other cycles and autos kept flashing by.

"You can get out now, sir. We're very close to the French border. With a little luck you should be in the French town of Metz before dawn. It's only about twenty kilometres from here, northeast."

"You're not coming with me?" he asked, with a startled look.

"No sir," I said. "You'd better give me back my colonel's jacket and hat. Sorry, sir—I'll need them."

"I suppose this wouldn't be a good time to ask what in the name of Christ you're doing here?" he said.

"No sir, this would not be a good time."

"You know the penalty for desertion?"

I found it difficult to answer for a moment, and then managed to say, "Yes sir, I do."

"You're not a coward, Peachy—that's for sure. I don't want you to disobey an order . . . so I'm not going to order you."

"Thank you, sir."

As he stepped a few feet away, to get out of the lights from passing cars while he changed costumes, I imagined the look on Annie's face when she saw that I did come back tonight and how happy she'd be. I pictured her standing in her doorway, smiling with tears, then hugging me, then taking my hand and leading me into her apartment. Then, for some stupid reason, I started fantasizing about the officers she must have slept with in order to keep the rapist, General Gruner, away from her. I pictured her standing naked with someone else . . . then making love with someone else. I tried to stop these thoughts—I tried, but I couldn't stop. When I pictured another man lying naked with her and being inside her, it hurt so much, until I finally realised that I was jealous of men that she probably hated. Then I realised how much I loved Annie.

Captain Harrington handed me my colonel's jacket and hat. He looked at me in a tender, almost fatherly way, and said, "How long do you think you can keep this up, Peachy? You know it's only a matter of time, don't you?"

"Yes sir, I know that."

I took the Lugar out of my briefcase and handed it to him.

"You may need this, sir. There are only seven bullets in it. I suggest you hold it in your left hand, just in case you need to salute anyone."

He took my hand and held it for a few seconds.

"-'Hair Nose Harrington,' huh?"

"I'm sorry, sir."

"That's all right—I've heard it, you know. It's not a bad song." Then he said, "Thank you for saving my life, Paul."

With a big grin I said, "You're welcome, sir."

"By the way, Peachy, where on earth did you get such a fantastic idea for getting me out of prison?"

"*Twelfth Night,* sir, by William Shakespeare. I had two lines in it at the Milwaukee Players."

He squeezed my hand and started walking toward the woods. Then he stopped and looked back.

"And thank you for the duck, Peachy."

I waited until I saw him disappear, then quickly shut the facing of the headlight, got onto my cycle, made a U-turn, and headed back to Karlsruhe.

After I left the outskirts of Saarbrücken, I raced through the countryside and heard Captain Harrington's words repeating in my head like a record on a phonograph: "You're not a coward, Peachy . . . You're not a coward." It made me so happy that I started singing "Hair Nose Harrington" to any nightingales who might be listening. I began figuring how long it would take before I'd see Annie again.

NINETEEN

⌒

I ARRIVED AT THE MOTORRAD PARKHAUS JUST AS THE church bells announced midnight. After I parked the cycle, I looked to see if there was a guard watching, but there wasn't. If there were a guard, he was probably sleeping. I walked into the locker room and quietly returned the riding jacket, goggles, and cap where I had found them and got out as quickly as I could.

I walked to the rear of Annie's apartment building, with my briefcase in hand. I was only wearing my trousers, boots, and an undershirt. I knew I should have put my colonel's jacket and hat back on, but I was too tired and too anxious to see Annie to care about taking any more precautions. Dumb, of course.

I climbed the backstairs and knocked softly on Annie's door. I thought she might be asleep, but she opened the door after only a few knocks. She smiled and tears came to her eyes. She took my hand and led me into her apartment, placed my briefcase on a table, and stood next to me. The love in her eyes surrounded me. I kissed her mouth and tasted the sweetness and warmth of her lips again.

"I need to take a bath, Annie."

"Would you like to take a swim?"

"I certainly would. Do you have a swimming pool in your backyard?"

"Yes, I do. Take off those things while I get something for you to wear."

When she came back she wrapped me into one of her robes, a little tight, of course, but it worked.

"And here are some sandals," she said. "They'll be a little tight, but you have small feet."

She led the way down the back stairway, with me in Annie's bathrobe and sandals, trying not to trip and hoping that no one from the building would pass by. Annie laughed when she saw me tiptoeing so carefully.

We got outside and walked about a hundred yards into a small wooded area, and there I saw a narrow stream with fresh water flowing past us. Annie took off her lavender robe and waded into the stream.

"Allez, allez," she called out. I suddenly understood French. I took off the robe and sandals and waded into the stream. The water was cold but not freezing, and we splashed each other for a few seconds. When I felt soft earth under my feet I laid myself down carefully, face up, held my nose, and let the cold water flow over my head, washing away the tension of the night. I felt safe, at least for now. And I was with Annie.

When we got back to her apartment, she dried me off with a big towel and led me to her kitchen, where she pulled out a bottle of red wine from a cupboard. She must have opened the bottle before she knew for sure if I was going to come back.

"Sit down, sweetheart," she said. "Are you hungry? I'm sure you must be. I have some cold cuts."

"Just the wine will be wonderful."

We sat at her kitchen table and I sipped my glass of wine slowly, looking at her tender face, remembering all the crazy thoughts that had flown through my head only an hour ago, when I realised how she must have hated the naked men I was jealous of, and why she thought of herself as a whore, and how stupid I was to be angry and . . .

"Can you tell me what happened tonight?" she asked politely, as if she knew she was interrupting my soliloquy.

". . . I realised how much I love you," I said.

Tears came to her eyes again, but she didn't say anything.

"Were you ever in love?" I asked.

She shook her head no.

"Didn't you ever have a boyfriend in school?"

"One Christmas—when I was seventeen," she said, as she wiped her eyes with the corner of her lavender wrap—"I went on a sleigh ride with some of my friends from school. There was a sweet boy, named Jean-Luc, and he was very handsome with wavy dark hair, but he was so shy. He kept looking at me and smiling while everyone else was laughing and singing rounds of children's songs and drinking beer as we rode through the snow. But when Jean-Luc saw me shiver from the cold, he came over and put his arm around me, and after three or four minutes he kissed me. That was my only kiss. I was raped by General Gruner six months later . . . and he didn't even kiss me."

I got up and wiped away some of her tears. Then I sat

on her lap. "Am I too heavy for you?" I asked.

"Never," she said.

"Does General Gruner ever come back to bother you?"

"No. The swine was sent to take command of the Russian front, and the day after he arrived he got his leg and one hand blown off. I cheered so loud when I heard the news. I went to Le Petit Bedon that night and shared a bottle of Champagne with Jamy. I got so drunk that he had to drive me home."

I kissed Annie as tenderly as I could. "There—now you've had two kisses—Jean-Luc's and mine."

She hugged me and whispered in my ear, "*Je t'aime.*" I said, "I tame you too."

"Oh my," she said, "you speak perfect French."

By now it was 1:00 a.m., and I thought I had better leave. As much as I liked Joseph, I took it for granted that he had to report to Colonel Steinig each day, so that the colonel would know where I went, who I was with, and how long I stayed. I didn't blame Joseph for that—that was his job—but I was thinking of Captain Harrington and my masquerade as Colonel von Rieger and thought I had better leave after spending "a pleasant evening with Mademoiselle Breton."

I didn't want to put on my colonel's jacket again, but I

knew I had to. I asked Annie to come downstairs with me and kiss me good night at the front door, so that Joseph could see that I had spent the evening with her. Annie didn't ask me to explain—she simply put on her bathrobe and a pair of slippers.

We walked down one flight of stairs and stepped outside. I exaggerated looking for the Mercedes. Joseph flashed the headlights lights once to show that he was waiting. Annie and I didn't have to "play act" kissing good night.

"Are you going to take me to the grand ball on Thursday?" she asked.

"Of course."

"And dance with me?"

"Of course," I said, "if I can get away from the Kaiser's wife. I hear she's a very strong woman with an iron grip."

"So am I," she said, and kissed me once more.

I got into the Mercedes, waved good-bye, and we drove away. It had been more than a good night's work.

TWENTY

WHEN I FINISHED BREAKFAST THE NEXT MORNING,
Colonel Steinig's lieutenant asked if I would please join
the colonel in his office. Steinig had a strange look on his
face when I walked in.

"I have some news for you, Harry . . . our famous prisoner, Captain Harrington, has escaped."

*Don't give anything away . . . don't overact . . . no
pretending to be shocked.*

"Go on," I said.

"Someone by the name of 'Colonel von Rieger' came to see him last night. He knew exactly which cell Harrington was in, visited with him for only fifteen minutes, and then left. His cycle driver was also with him. This morning the cell was empty."

"Do you know Colonel von Rieger," I asked.

"I've never heard of him . . . have you?"

Deep in thought . . . stay deep in thought . . . you're prepared . . . don't rush it.

"Did von Rieger give a first name?" I asked.

"No! What the hell difference would that make?" he answered, more impatiently than he'd ever spoken to me.

"Did he wear an eye patch?" I asked.

Steinig was flabbergasted. "How on earth did you know that?"

"Because 'Karl von Rieger,' alias 'Karl Joseph Landmann,' is an American officer whose actual name is Karl Schneider. He works in American Intelligence. His favourite disguise is to wear an eye patch. With a hat and eye patch, people can't seem to remember his face."

"How do you know all of this?"

"Because I've met him. On several occasions. He's clever. I think he's also a show-off who's too full of himself, but he gets away with it . . . as you can see."

"How could he know where Harrington was? Even which cell he was in?"

"If it was Karl Schneider—and I'm sure it was—it would be child's play. After they captured Harrington, your brilliant officers took him to Saarbrücken, which is only twenty-five kilometres from enemy lines and which has an old prison that's almost ready to fall apart. All this he would know. How he knew that Harrington was in cell fourteen . . . I don't know. *But*—if I were him, I would probably come to Saarbrücken very often, dressed as a farmer or a workman, and frequent the local saloons. I assure you he'd be very good at acting a little tipsy with one of the prison guards, who just wants to relax and have a few drinks after his shift is over."

"You make it sound so simple"

"It is simple—if you're talented. And he is."

"I'm sorry if I spoke rudely before—it was very discouraging when I heard that he had escaped."

"I wouldn't worry about Captain Harrington, Viktor—he's just a company commander. What did he tell us?—that the main attack would come from Switzerland? I don't believe it. It's possible, of course, but I think he was lying. Anyway, if you catch a general, then I might be of some use."

"I'm glad you're on our side, Harry."

The next day, everyone in the castle was scurrying in and out of the ballroom, cleaning and polishing everything in sight, because Colonel Steinig was giving a ball in honour of Kaiser Wilhelm II and his wife, Augusta Victoria.

I had intended to pick up Annie at her apartment so she wouldn't get lost in the shuffle of all the dignitaries who were invited, but Colonel Steinig asked if I would please join the reception line. I asked Joseph to bring Annie.

That evening, as the chamber orchestra was playing Strauss, I was standing in a short line, greeting generals and their wives, and a prince or two, with one or two princesses. I pretended that it was like a wedding in Milwaukee, and I mumbled little pleasantries: "An honour, sir." "How wonderful to meet you, madam," or whatever else came to mind. But I had no idea what you were supposed to say to a Kaiser and his wife. I was more concerned with seeing Annie and kept looking out for her.

"Here come the Kaiser and his wife," Steinig whispered to me.

"Remember, don't kiss the Kaiser and shake the wife's hand," Steinig said with a laugh.

"Well, that depends how handsome he is."

As insane as it may sound, I still had to remind myself not to kiss the Kaiser's hand and shake the hand of his wife.

As they approached, Steinig did the introductions.

"Your highness, may I present Col. Harry Stroller, whom I know you've heard so much about . . . Colonel Stroller, may I present Friedrich Wilhelm Viktor Albert von Hohenzollern . . . our illustrious Kaiser."

The Kaiser stuck out his hand. I shook it (thank goodness) and said, "What a great honour for me." He nodded and moved on. What a stuck-up prig.

Then Augusta Victoria approached. She gave me a warm smile and put out her hand. I kissed it.

"What a thrill to meet you," I said, and then I bit my tongue, wishing that I hadn't said, 'thrill to meet you,' as if I were talking to a silent screen actress. But she was very gracious, thanked me, and moved on.

I saw Annie enter the ballroom. She was prettier than all of the other women in the room. She wore a white gown, white gloves, high heels, and just a tiny blush of rouge on her cheeks. Her hair wasn't lacquered or rolled or puffed . . . it was just natural. I wanted to run up and kiss her, but I thought I might get thrown out. *Later, Private Peachy . . . hold your horses.*

I walked up to Annie, took her hand, kissed it, and

glided her into the waltz that was playing. I pretended that I was whispering something, but actually I was kissing her ear as we danced.

I danced three waltzes in a row with Annie. When the music stopped, we stood on the floor, waiting for the music to begin again.

"You are . . . a very beautiful woman," I said.

"Thank you, dear."

Then I realised that we had better not just stand there, looking at each other and waiting for the next dance, or people might get the right idea. We moved to the refreshment tables.

Annie had Champagne and I, stupidly, looked for "Sincere." But of course, they only had German wines. Germany was trying to annihilate the French, so why would they display French wines. I settled for a German white. It was good, but not as good as "Sincere."

Colonel Steinig called out "Harry!" and walked up to us.

"I can't stall for you any longer," he said. "She wants her dance."

"The Kaiser's wife?" I asked, as panic shot through my heart.

"No, the Countess von Oppersdorf. You promised her a dance, Harry, remember? She's standing at the edge of the dance floor with the count and a few friends."

I saw the countess smiling at me. Then she waved. I waved back and signalled, "I'll be right there."

I put my wine glass down and said, "Would you take care of this young lady for me, Viktor?"

"Both the count and his young lieutenant have been waiting very patiently to have a dance with Annie," he said.

"They had better flip a coin," I said, "because she has only one free dance left."

"I don't think I can ask the count to flip a coin, Harry."

"Oh well," I said, as I looked at Annie, "then let the count have the dance—the young lieutenant is too handsome."

I squeezed Annie's hand and walked over to the count and countess as the music started up again. We spoke only in German.

"Harry," the count said, "my wife thought you were avoiding her."

"I always save the best things for last, sir," I said, and then I kissed the countess's hand.

"Oh, dear—I have to compete with that?" the count asked. The count looked at the handsome young lieutenant beside him.

"Harry, this is my aide, Lt. Erich von Hebbel."

Lieutenant Hebbel put out his hand and gushed, "A great pleasure to meet you, sir."

I shook hands with him, thanked him, and turned to the countess.

"And now, my dear Countess . . . I think the time has come. I've been waiting all evening."

"Oh dear! I'm not very good," the countess said, as I led her onto the dance floor. This very sweet, very charming lady, was also very heavy and an exceptionally rotten dancer. Every time I tripped over her feet, I tried to make it appear as if it were my fault.

"I'm sorry, Countess—you're so good that sometimes I can't keep up with you. Are you tired?"

"No, not at all," she said. "Are you?"

"No, no—not at all," I said. "This is so much fun."

After we danced for several minutes, I noticed that the countess was sweating.

"Are you thirsty, Countess?" I asked.

She hesitated and said, "Well . . ."

"Oh, please—I can take a hint. You don't have to be polite with me. Shall we both get a cool drink?"

"That would be nice. Thank you, Colonel Stroller. You're such a gentleman."

We walked over to the refreshment table where some friends of the countess were drinking and laughing. I

ordered a glass of Champagne for the countess and one
for myself. As I waited for our drinks, and while the
countess made small talk with her friends, I looked for
Annie. She was in the middle of the floor, dancing with
the count and laughing at whatever silly jokes he liked to
tell. I heard someone call, "Harry!"

I turned and saw Colonel Steinig standing next to
some officer, waving at me to join them. When I arrived,
Steinig said, "Harry, good news! Your old friend, General
von Sieghardt, says that he owes you money from two
years ago when you both made a bet."

The general gave me a cold stare.

"Hermann, you are an honest man, I must say," Steinig
said. "Did you think he wouldn't remember, Harry?"

Fire raced through my body.

*Start thinking, Peachy. Don't panic. What would
Stroller do?*

"You've changed a great deal, Hermann," I said.

"Who is this man?" General von Sieghardt asked.

Steinig looked at the general and then at me.

"This is Colonel . . . I'm sorry, Hermann," Steinig said,
". . . I'm afraid I don't understand what you mean."

Countess von Oppersdorf walked up, holding two
glasses of Champagne.

"Harry, your Champagne," she said, and handed me

my glass.

"Thank you, Countess," I said. "Hermann, do you know the Countess von Oppersdorf?"

"We're cousins, Harry," the Countess said, with a very stern face. "But we never got along, did we, Hermann?"

The general just kept staring at me.

"Do you understand this situation, Harry?" Steinig asked.

"It's very confusing," I answered.

"Hermann and I rarely see each other," the Countess said. "My cousin is always so busy—not even time for a short visit when my sister was dying."

"Excuse me, Countess . . . May we step onto the terrace, gentlemen?" Steinig interrupted. "Harry? . . . Herm ann? . . . Please."

"Yes, certainly," I said.

"Countess, will you excuse us for a moment?" Steinig asked.

"You see what I mean?" the Countess asked. "Hermann hasn't even been here two minutes, and he disrupts the whole evening. Don't be too long, Harry—we never finished our dance."

"I wish you hadn't been so thirsty, Countess," I said.

General von Sieghardt walked onto the terrace. I looked at the Countess, feeling great fondness for her now. I said,

"Thank you for bringing my Champagne."

"Excuse us, Countess," Steinig said.

When I walked onto the terrace and looked at General Sieghardt, I felt like a child caught playing with matches. I wanted to run away, but there was nowhere to run.

"Gentlemen," Steinig said, "won't you please sit? I would prefer not to attract attention if it can be helped."

The general and I sat on the low stone wall that surrounded the terrace. I positioned myself where I could look through the French doors and get glimpses of Annie.

"No nonsense—who are you?" Steinig asked, looking directly at me.

I thought of Captain Harrington. He had looked at me in such a tender, almost fatherly way before we said good-bye. *"How long do you think you can keep this up, Peachy? You know it's only a matter of time, don't you?" "Yes sir, I know that."*

"I'm an American soldier," I answered.

Colonel Steinig looked stunned. "What is your rank?" he asked.

"Private."

The general's eyes shot daggers at me.

"Go on," Steinig said. He was colder than I had ever heard him. I looked through the French doors and saw Annie.

Tell the truth, Peachy.

"Two weeks ago, there was a general attack at six in the morning," I said. "My two very dear friends were shot in the head before they even got out of the trench. When I saw them lying on the ground, with their eyes open, I was terrified. Our whole company rushed up the fire steps and I followed, but when I heard the machine guns and saw all the bodies dropping around me, I ran into some woods about a quarter of a mile away. I was captured by a German patrol. A sergeant, who had a head like a pig's, ordered his squad to shoot me. Because I spoke German, I was able to trick the sergeant and his men into thinking that I was a German officer. I ordered them to take me to their commanding officer. I didn't even know what I was going to do when I got there, but I worked it out on the way to the headquarters of Capt. Stefan Simmel. Shortly after I arrived, you spoke to him on the telephone, Viktor."

Steinig was puzzled—not sympathetic, just puzzled.

"How did you know about Colonel Stroller?" he asked.

"Harry Stroller was captured—or rather, he gave himself up the morning before. Because I spoke German, I was asked to stay with him through the night and try to get information from him. I talked to him in German for almost an hour and then he suddenly spoke to me in perfect English. He was very kind."

General Sieghardt looked like a frustrated fisherman who was finally about to haul in a largemouth bass.

"He gave himself up?" Sieghardt shouted.

"Yes sir."

"Did your great new friend happen to tell you why he gave himself up?" Sieghardt shouted.

Don't lie . . . tell this bastard the truth.

"He said it was all over in Germany—but you didn't know it yet."

Now General Sieghardt looked like a dragon, as he exhaled through his nose.

"And that's all?" Steinig asked.

"Yes sir."

General von Sieghardt took out his watch, which hung on a beautiful gold chain.

"I give you seven minutes. If you don't tell the truth by then, you will be dragged from here and shot immediately."

I looked at my "friend," Colonel Steinig.

"Do you believe me, Viktor?"

"Not one word," he answered.

I was at a complete loss, but for some reason my panic lessened. I even felt relieved. I looked through the French doors and saw Annie laughing. She was with another group of guests, who were standing around the Count von Oppersdorf. He was probably telling more silly jokes. I was glad I didn't see Annie dancing with the handsome young lieutenant.

"Whoever you are," Steinig said, "I suggest that you speak very soon. I can assure you that the general will stick to his plan."

General von Sieghardt was looking at his watch, timing me.

"Who are you?" Steinig asked.

I paused for just a second, and then I answered as if I had just heard the question.

"I'm a spy."

"For who?" Steinig asked.

"You mean for 'whom,' don't you, Viktor?"

Now I got a smile. Steinig nodded his remembrance.

"For America," I said. "Stroller was captured three weeks ago by the British. They knew he was working for Germany. They also knew that he was known, personally, by only a few people. I was asked to try the switch . . . pass myself off as Stroller, because of my background."

"What is your background?" Steinig asked.

"American Intelligence. I had a German father and mother. I also used to work in the theatre, Viktor . . . several years ago. Remember?"

By the look in his eyes I could see that Colonel Steinig was hearing everything he had hoped for.

"Who was your contact here?" Steinig asked me.

"I didn't have a contact here . . . he was in England."

Steinig was lost in thought for a moment; then he asked, "Did you get Captain Harrington out of prison?"

"Yes."

"How?"

"In your report this morning, did they mention a motorcycle driver with goggles?"

Steinig smiled. "That was quite brilliant," he said. "Harrington was the driver and you were Colonel Reiger."

"No—on the way out I was the driver with goggles and Harrington was Colonel Reiger, with the eye patch."

"Brilliant," Steinig said again.

I looked at General Sieghardt, who obviously didn't think I was so brilliant.

"What is your actual rank?" Steinig asked.

"I'm a colonel."

"And what is your real name?"

"Wally Murdock."

"Thank you . . . Colonel Murdock," Steinig said.

"May I please ask a favour, Viktor."

Steinig looked at the general, who shook his head no.

"That would depend, really, on what the favour is," Steinig said to me.

"It would depend on nothing!" the general burst in. "This man is a spy."

"I know, sir," Steinig said. "I meant only—under the unusual circumstances . . ."

General Sieghardt got up and walked over to Colonel Steinig.

"The unusual circumstances are that not only is he a confessed spy but he has made fools of a great many people—yourself included. I certainly don't intend . . ."

"Shut your mouth, Hermann!" I said.

The general couldn't believe what I had said. He looked at me with his mouth slightly open.

"Approximately two hundred people in the ballroom believe that I am Stroller. Would you like to see Harry Stroller dragged out of here, screaming hysterically? Or would you rather see me run inside, calling you a madman when you start shooting?"

General von Sieghardt stared at me. Then he looked at the nearest guard, who was not that near.

"I don't say that you won't be able to explain," I said,

"but it won't be easy. In any case, you lose a great hero."

Now it was von Sieghardt who was lost in thought.

"You have the floor, Harry . . . or whatever your name is," Steinig said. "Please don't be too extravagant."

"Ten minutes," I said.

Colonel Steinig glanced into the ballroom. He saw Annie looking for me.

"I knew you were a romantic," Steinig said, "but this is beyond my imagination."

"It's not an extravagant request," I said.

"No," Steinig answered. "Under the circumstances—it's not very extravagant."

"NO!" Von Sieghardt said.

"YES, General," Steinig said. "I think, yes."

The general stared at Steinig, but Steinig stared right back.

"I really think so, Hermann. We need heroes right now."

The general didn't answer.

"Shall we go in, gentlemen?" Steinig asked. Then he put his arm around mine and led the three of us into the ballroom.

I think my absence for such a long time had Annie worried, but when she saw me the worry disappeared.

When I stood close to her she asked, "Now where were

you?" the way she might have asked a little child who had stayed away from home too long. Tears came to her eyes.

"Why are you crying?" I asked.

"Because I love you, and I was worried that they wanted to send you on another assignment far away from me."

I needed to hold her. I put my arm around her waist and began dancing to some ballad that the orchestra was playing. I think it was an American song, but I don't remember the name.

"You look very handsome tonight," she said.

"You've had too much Champagne," I said.

She looked at my eyes, where she could always see what I was feeling.

"What were you thinking just now?" she asked.

"How happy I am to be with you."

"Wouldn't it be nice if we took a short holiday and drove into the country? Just the two of us?" she asked.

"Yes, that would be wonderful," I said.

". . . And we could stop at some little inn and drink the country wine and sleep under a fluffy quilt, with a small candle burning in the corner all night?"

"Yes."

"Will you take me to France after the war?"

"Yes."

"Do you promise?"

"If I can still dance and make love with you and drink 'Sincere' . . . yes, I promise."

"I'd like to live on a farm someday," she said. "Maybe not all of the time, but for a while. Do you think you would like that?"

"Yes, I think I would."

"Why are you leaving me?" she asked.

I tried to look away so that she couldn't read my eyes, but she did see them.

"You have to leave, don't you?" she asked.

"Yes, I do."

"When?" she asked.

"Now."

"It must be very important."

"It is," I answered.

"Will it be for long?"

"No . . . I don't think so. Not too long."

"Is there anything I can do?"

"No. Thank you. You're always so kind."

"I just want you to be happy," she said. "And I don't want you to worry about me. I'm sure you have enough on your mind. You are happy, aren't you, dear?"

"Yes, I am . . . very happy."

TWENTY-ONE

⁓

VICTOR STEINIG ALLOWED ME TO GO TO MY ROOM FOR a minute. I was accompanied by three guards. I picked up this notebook and my fountain pen and the package that I had wrapped my American uniform in. Then I was taken to an old jail in Karlsruhe. I think it was once a stable. It looked onto a large, open field, where I suppose the horses had been taken out to exercise.

My cell had a small table and a cot, plus a large pot for me to relieve myself in. A guard came into my cell and placed a pot of coffee and a cup on the table. I'm sure that was Colonel Steinig's doing. As the guard left, he saluted me.

I wrote in my notebook until dawn. I certainly didn't want to waste my last hours sleeping. It's six in the morning now. To my surprise, Colonel Steinig came to see me.

"It's chilly this morning," he said.

I just nodded. I think he wanted to say something that sounded normal. He lit a cigarette for himself and then held out the pack to me.

"Would you care for a cigarette, Harry?"

The warmth in his smile came back when he thought he was talking to Harry Stroller again.

"No, thank you very much, Viktor—I don't smoke."

"Would you like me to have Annie brought here, so you can say good-bye?"

"Oh, no. Thank you, but no. There is one favour I'd like to ask."

"Yes?"

"Would you please send Joseph to see me? . . . my driver, Joseph Tausk? There's something I'd like to give him."

Viktor smiled.

"Joseph brought me here this morning. He's waiting outside. I think he wanted to see you."

Viktor motioned to one of the guards and told him to unlock the cell door. Viktor stepped out and spoke to his lieutenant, who was standing nearby. After a second or two, Viktor and Joseph walked into my cell.

"I'll say good-bye, Harry," Viktor said. "I'm glad that I had the pleasure of meeting you."

As we shook hands, I said, "You're a good friend, Viktor."

He smiled, looking slightly relieved, called for the guard to unlock the cell door, and he left.

After he was gone I took Joseph's hand. He looked terribly shaken at seeing me in jail. I'm sure he knew I was going to be shot in a short while.

"Joseph, would you do me a very great favour?" I asked.

"Of course, sir."

I took my notebook and held it out to Joseph.

"Would you hand this notebook, personally, to Mademoiselle Breton?"

"Of course, sir," he said. He was trembling a little.

"Good-bye, my dear friend," I said, as I embraced him.

"Good-bye, sir," he said.

I suddenly remembered something.

"Oh, wait! Joseph—excuse me—I need to write just

one more thing."

I tore out a piece of paper from my notebook and wrote one line. Then I placed it on top of the first page:

"My dearest . . . when I finally found you, I fell in love over my ears."

NOVEMBER 28, 1918

Dear Captain Harrington:

Paul Peachy requested that whenever the war was over I should send this notebook to you. The only address he gave me was: Captain John Harrington, Rhinelander, Wisconsin. With all my heart I hope that it reaches you.

Sincerely,
Annie Breton

ACKNOWLEDGEMENTS

For whatever simplicity of language I have achieved, I thank my two mentors: Ernest Hemingway and Jean Renoir.